namako

sea cucumber

なまこ

namako|

sea cucumber

A NOVEL BY

Linda

Watanabe

McFerrin

COFFEE HOUSE PRESS

Coffee House Press is supported in part by a grant provided by the Minnesota State Arts Board, through an appropriation by the Minnesota State Legislature, and in part by a grant from the National Endowment for the Arts. Special funding for this title was provided by the Star Tribune Foundation. Significant support has also been provided by the McKnight Foundation; Lannan Foundation; Jerome Foundation; Target Stores, Dayton's, and Mervyn's by the Dayton Hudson Foundation; General Mills Foundation; The St. Paul Companies; Butler Family Foundation; Honeywell Foundation; James R. Thorpe Foundation; Dain Bosworth Foundation; Pentair, Inc.; the Peter & Madeleine Martin Foundation; the law firm of Schwegman, Lundberg, Woessner & Kluth, P.A.; and many individual donors. To you and our many readers across the country, we send our thanks for your continuing support.

Coffee House Press books are available to the trade through our primary distributor, Consortium Book Sales & Distribution, 1045 Westgate Drive, Saint Paul, MN 55114. For personal orders, catalogs, or other information, write to: Coffee House Press, 27 N. 4th Street, Suite 400, Minneapolis, MN 55401.

library of congress CIP data
Watanabe McFerrin, Linda,
    Namako : sea cucumber / Linda Watanabe McFerrin. —1st ED.
        p.   cm.
    ISBN 1-56689-075-6 (ALK. PAPER)
    1. Japanese Americans—Fiction.   I. Title.
    PS3573.A7987N3   1998
    813'.54—dc21   98-21156
                                                               CIP

10   9   8   7   6   5   4   3   2   1
first edition / first printing

CONTENTS

author acknowledgements I was not alone in creating this book. It is the work of many hands, from Michael Rubin, now deceased, my instructor at San Fransico State University, who inspired the first vignettes, to Charles and Gail Entrekin, Jamie Woolery, Carla Kandinsky, and the other poets who taught me how writers write; from my characters, Gene, Sara, Ellen, Samuel, Mimi, and Gray and the others with whom I have lived all these years to Kee, Richard, and Lowry who slogged through early versions of the novel.

Three women stand out for special recognition—my Graces in relation to this project—Alice Acheson, Victoria Shoemaker, and Elaine Petrocelli, as do my clients and cohorts in the apparel industry who heartened me immeasurably in the pursuit of this seemingly unrelated enterprise, and my friends and students—Lory, Susan, Ann, Toni, Mary Brent, Colleen, Marianne, Jacqueline, Michelle, and so many others who share the love of words.

I must also acknowledge previous editors, my publisher, and the team at Coffee House Press for believing in my work and having patience with my long, and often convoluted, sentence constructions.

Most especially I want to thank my friend, Katsu Miyata, who helped me through the Japanese text, which I found difficult—if there are any errors, they are mine, not his—, and Lowry McFerrin, for continuing to hold back the tsunami.

for

Amelia,

Richard,

& Paul

Who goes with Fergus?

Who will go drive with Fergus now,
And pierce the deep wood's woven shade,
And dance upon the level shore?
Young man, lift up your russet brow,
And lift your tender eyelids, maid,
And brood on hopes and fear no more . . .

—W.B. YEATS

yurei yashiki

ghost house

1

naisho |
secrets

The childhood I remember was full of secrets. Really, they were lies.

For example, it was a lie that we went to Japan because my grandmother was ill. The real reason was that my father, Gene, was having an affair, and my mother, Sara, had threatened to leave him. Sara's laughing red mouth and her courage were also a lie. She was always afraid that someone would die—something that happened to her again and again.

For a while, almost every word that came out of my mouth was a lie. Perhaps this was because that is what I saw all around me. But I lied so well that nobody knew. So my lies became secrets, too.

2

shashin |
picture

I will tell you, first, that I wasn't lonely when I was a child.
But that is a lie. It was also one of my secrets.

When I was nine years old I came across a black-and-white
picture on one of the text-filled pages of the "P" volume of my
parents' encyclopedia. It was a photograph of a painting by
Pablo Picasso. The people in the painting were circus perform-
ers. They were a strange group of people—a family. They
looked very flat in that black-and-white photograph—gray
objects in a gray landscape. They did not look at one another.
Each one appeared to have drifted toward his own horizon.
Their relationship seemed circumstantial, almost an accident.

My favorite person in this picture was the girl. She wasn't
pretty at all. She had small, adolescent breasts. Everything
about her looked awkward. Her hands and feet had a simian
quality. One day, I took my little pointed sewing scissors and
cut the picture out of the encyclopedia. Then, I cut the girl
out from the picture. I called the girl "Fergus" and gave her a

home in a bluish-white airmail envelope that I had taken from Sara, my mother. The photograph of the Picasso painting looked just as it had before, except now the girl was no longer in it. I used hard paste to glue the altered picture into my composition book. No one ever noticed it missing.

That same year, my parents, Sara and Gene, decided that our family would move to Japan.

I had only a vague idea of where Japan was and had never met our Japanese grandmother who was Sara's mother and who, they told us, was dying. I'd seen pictures of her, though. Sara's mother was from Japan. Gene's family was from Scotland. Both of Gene's parents were dead. So was Sara's father. So Hanabe, Sara's mother, was our only grandparent. The woman in Sara's photos did not look like my idea of a grandmother. She looked a lot like Sara—fair-skinned, dark-haired, and thin—only taller. She seemed too young to be dying. She wore mannish suits and ties.

Sara loved photographs and she loved to take them. We had albums full of them. We had pictures of Grandmother taken by Sara, pictures of Gene, pictures of me, pictures of my siblings: Samuel, Mimi, and Gray. We even had pictures of Sara taking pictures. And Sara always had pictures made of the pictures. She had reprints made and tucked them into her letters to Grandmother. Sara wrote a lot of letters—at least two a week. She wrote them on onionskin so that they'd weigh less and cost less money to mail. But the letters were still bulky by the time she was finished. They were strange-looking too— long, vertical lines of Japanese characters, mysterious glyphs waterfalling down pages and pages of thin, see-through paper. Sara, who is half-British and half-Japanese, always wrote to her mother in Japanese, although her best language is English. I think she did this to keep the contents a secret. I wondered if those letters were full Sara's sorrow and happiness. I loved handling them, lifting the well-stuffed envelopes and imagining what they contained. They were the closest I ever got to her soul.

I didn't really believe we were going to Japan because Grandmother was ill or dying or anything like that. As I saw it, we were going because of the red-haired woman who was in the kitchen with Gene one morning after one of my parents' big parties. The woman was one of their overnight guests. Sometimes their friends would dance too hard or drink too much and not make it home.

That morning Gene was wearing mismatched flannel pajamas, and his short brown hair was sticking straight up because he had just gotten up. The tops of his pajamas had pictures of snowshoes and skis tossed about on them. They were a Christmas gift from all of us. The bottoms were a faded blue-and-red plaid. They'd been a birthday present two years before. Over these he had on a silk paisley robe. That was a gift from Sara.

The red-haired woman was wearing one of Sara's robes— the black, silk kimono with a gold Chinese dragon embroidered on the back. Gene had just handed her his favorite hangover cure—a half-glass of Worcestershire sauce with a raw egg floating on top.

"Hey, Ellen," Gene greeted me when I entered the kitchen.

My parents called all of us by our first names. So we thought it was fine to call them by theirs.

"Hey, Gene," I replied, "I came in for cornflakes. Can you reach for the cornflakes, please?" Gene kept the cornflakes on the highest shelf of the cupboard where only someone of his height could reach them. He kept them there so that he could control their consumption. Usually, he ate things like eggs and pancakes and hash browns for breakfast. On those rare occasions when he wanted cold cereal, he hated to find the box empty. He was so preoccupied with the woman that he handed over the cornflakes without a remark.

The red-haired woman was making a big deal of studying the contents of the glass that Gene had given her.

"Swallow the egg in one gulp," Gene advised.

"Your father claims this is going to save me," she laughed, talking to me. "I don't know. I don't know."

She shook her head and her red hair bounced, and I could see why Gene was probably crazy about her. I sat in the kitchen, ate my cornflakes and watched Gene and the woman drink their eggy hangover chasers in front of the sink. I saw how Gene put his hand on the woman's back and how she reached up and drew an imaginary line on his whiskery morning jaw with her fingertips. His face brushed lightly against her red hair, and his hand moved down her spine, tracing the shape of the dragon. Then he remembered me sitting there and looked over his shoulder with a bashful grin like I was supposed to understand just what he was up to. It was as if he were daring me not to say anything. Later that day, when Sara finally got up, I told her I thought Gene was in love with that beautiful, red-haired woman.

"I want to have red hair," I added.

I knew I was right about Gene and the woman because Sara's eyes narrowed and her mouth gathered up in a pout.

"Your complexion is wrong for red hair," she said simply.

Sara had a very short fuse. That night at dinner, somewhere between the shrimp cocktail and steak, she confronted Gene about the red-haired woman, whose name was Ceci. Ceci was their mutual friend. Sara said Gene could do what he liked; she'd take the children and move to Japan. It was quite a surprise. Sara had never even suggested going to Japan before that, but she never made idle threats.

"What makes you think that Ceci and I are involved anyway, Sara?" Gene asked defensively, swallowing steak.

"I have my spies," Sara replied not-so-cryptically, all but implicating me in a glance.

"Sara," Gene pleaded, sounding very dejected which was always the best way to deal with her, "you can't leave. I love you."

It sounded scripted to me. Gene was trying to win Sara over, but she turned on him and on us.

"All right," she said, "we'll all go together."

Gene couldn't argue that point.

Sara always got what she wanted.

So it was, in some way, my fault we moved.

When I heard that we were definitely going to Japan, I ran to my bedroom and slammed the door shut. I took Fergus out of her envelope. Using my scissors, I cut her up into tiny triangular pieces. Then, I glued the pieces all over a piece of white notebook paper. Then, I burned the paper. That was the end of Fergus.

We left for Japan that spring.

But first, because Sara was almost completely getting her way, Gene got to fulfill one of his dreams. Gene had this dream of taking his family on a discovery tour of the "Great Western Wilderness." Never mind that we weren't the traditional family, that we looked as all-American as a plate full of sushi. In pursuit of Gene's illusion, we all had to rattle around for the next few weeks, crammed into the green Chevy station wagon, through a series of national parks and small western towns. Gene was the amateur impresario. We were his troupe—the semihostile wife, and four ill-behaved kids. Six people was not a large family in the sixties. Some of my friends came from families of seven or eight. Sara had told us that, in contrast, couples in Japan rarely had more than two children. This made Mimi and Gray, the two youngest and therefore the two "extra" children, somewhat nervous.

"It's because the women are of slighter build in Japan," Sara explained. "You see, their hips are so narrow that childbearing is difficult."

It made sense. Sara always said things that could easily have been true.

"Then again, it could be because the country is smaller," she added. "Small country, small families. That's logical."

Sara kept us off balance like that. We never knew what to believe.

I had to wonder why, in our case, Sara had chosen not to favor her Japanese side and the preference for smaller families. She rarely did things without a good reason, but the reasons always seemed more like afterthoughts. The only child of a British journalist and a Japanese actress living in China, she'd spent most of her childhood in Catholic boarding schools. She must have been out of place there. She must have been lonely a lot. I guessed that was why she kept having children.

Sara told us she'd lost her first two babies in childbirth. If they had lived, we would have been a family of eight: two parents, six kids. The first two children, the ones she lost, were Andrew and Jeffrey. They would have been our older brothers. Jeffrey was born a few years before me with his umbilical cord wrapped around his neck like a collar. He was totally blue when he was born; he was dead. Andrew, who was really the oldest, was a miscarriage. Sara said she could see his small hands and feet when he flowed out of her in a sea of blood. She said his skin was so thin, she could almost see through him. Sara didn't want to forget these two, so she mentioned them often. We felt like they were always with us, a couple of spooky presences—one blue and one see-through—sharing the car seat or restaurant booth.

She'd say things like, "Today would be Andrew's twelfth birthday."

Gene didn't like it when Sara did this. He didn't like it when Sara said things that were strange. He'd squint at her closely, then lapse into silence.

So, I guess I was really the third child. My brother, Samuel, who was two years younger than I, was the fourth; Gray, a year younger than Samuel was fifth and Mimi, a year junior to Gray, was the sixth. But, Sara and Gene had four living children, and that was plenty.

We could all tell, that summer, that Gene was in over his head. He grew tired of the endless search for soft drinks and toilets, of the squabbles and tears. Generally, Sara efficiently handled the day-to-day struggles, leaving the high-profile problems to Gene. He had not expected the petty lows to which life can deteriorate in the constant presence of children. His dream had turned into a nightmare.

It began almost at once in Glacier National Park, high in the U.S.-Canadian Rockies. We were staying at Lake Mac-Donald Lodge on the western side of the park. It was spring, so the rivers were swollen from all of the snow-melt. Samuel and Gray hiked up to MacDonald Falls by themselves where they traded marbles with two other boys for the use of a couple of inner tubes with which to ride down the river. Steelies, puries, cat's eyes, pee wees and boulders went into the trade. Six-year-old Gray, terrified by the churning waters, abandoned the adventure, only to watch Samuel disappear downriver in a white-water spray. He did not emerge from the water. Gray came crying back to the lodge. For two terrible hours we hunted for Samuel with the help of the lodge personnel, rangers, and other park visitors. Samuel must have known he was in trouble when he finally materialized from the stand of spruce where he'd hidden in an attempt to scare Gray. Gene was furious; Sara in tears.

At that point I thought Gene would figure out that his great plan was a failure, but he can be really stubborn sometimes. So we traveled south across Montana by car and ended up in Yellowstone Park on the Montana-Wyoming border. That's where Mimi was stalked by a bear. We were picnicking on some boulders. Sara and Gene were discussing Sara's mother.

"She's tough and old-fashioned," Gene said. "The kids are not going to like her."

"They'll learn." Sara countered. "Especially Ellen; Mother will teach her strong values."

"If Ellen survives. She's already far too much like Hanabe."

"For you?"

"No, for you," Gene said softly. "It isn't your way."

"It works," Sara answered. "It's what Ellen needs."

No one noticed that Mimi was missing. At the time, in addition to eavesdropping, I was still trying to get over my disappointment over geysers. At Old Faithful, we had waited for hours with busloads of blond, blue-eyed people at a hole in the ground. Nothing happened. Gene shrugged his shoulders.

"Life is like that sometimes," he said.

"That's for sure," Sara seconded, and they both laughed mirthlessly.

The geysers just seemed like another big lie.

The park ranger who brought Mimi back to us told us that Mimi had tempted a bear with the wax paper wrapper from one of her peanut butter and jelly sandwiches. He'd rescued her from a rocky escarpment into which she had crawled to hide.

"Luckily it was a black bear," the ranger said. "It wasn't a grizzly, and that's a good thing. This little girl wouldn't be here if that bear was a grizzly. But, a black bear can kill a child, too. These bears get bold if people feed them," he cautioned. "Their natural fear of humans dissolves. Next thing you know we're picking up pieces. Don't feed the bears," he concluded.

Mimi said that the bear had simply approached her and barked. She said that it made a strange "woofing" noise. Then it had tried to take half of her sandwich. Mimi said that she'd tricked it, surrendering only the wrapper and part of the crust.

"That bear was my friend," she asserted. "He wouldn't hurt me."

"Right, Mimi," said Gene. "That bear would have clobbered you for your sandwich. Bears are wild things. They don't love as we do."

At his words, Mimi's eyes welled with tears.

"Fort Peck Reservoir," the boys laughed. "Hoover Dam. Mimi's going to cry."

Mimi stuffed the tears, burying her face in her old, yellow blanket. Gene and the boys could be brutal sometimes.

After leaving Yellowstone Park, we headed south for Death Valley National Monument. That was Gene's biggest mistake.

Death Valley is not a place to visit with four children in June. "'In the summer, the temperature in Death Valley can reach 134 degrees. It's one of the hottest places in the world. Just sitting in the shade in Death Valley on an average day, you can lose two gallons of water. If you lose one quart of body fluid you will get thirsty. If you lose one gallon, you will become tired and apathetic. Your blood will thicken. Your heart will strain. If you lose more water, you'll start to stumble. You will not be able to breathe very well. You will lose your power of speech. If you continue to lose body fluids, your tongue will swell. You'll probably take off your clothes to cool off, and this is the worst thing you can possibly do. Then your tongue will shrivel, your vision will blur and you won't be able to hear anymore. Bloody cracks will appear in your skin. Then you will die.'"

I was sharing this information with everyone in the car. We had the windows rolled down, and we were all stuck in our small pools of sweat to the station wagon's softening vinyl upholstery.

"'No one wants to die of thirst,'" I concluded, reading from a book that we had purchased at the Visitors' Center in Yellowstone National Park, "'so it isn't surprising that we avoid deserts, Death Valley among them.'"

Actually, I was really enjoying Death Valley. Funny-shaped plants called Joshua trees stuck up from the colorless land-scape like alien antennae. There were signs pointing toward ghost towns that didn't seem to exist. I saw two wild burros and a coyote when I was scanning the near-naked horizon.

"Fergus would have liked this," I said to myself, thinking that perhaps I had killed Fergus off too early.

Gene, however, was not amused by my performance and not too pleased with this part of the trip. He and Sara were in the midst of another fight. A horrible silence filled the car. It swelled like a boil between Sara and Gene. Sara had started this one.

"Gray wants to know the difference between a hotel and a motel," she announced unexpectedly while we were driving along.

"What did you tell him?" Gene asked.

"I told him hotels are for the rich people and motels are for people with children. He says he wants to stay in a hotel."

"He'll get his chance. There won't be motels in Japan."

"No motels. True. Too bad for you. You don't want to go to Japan."

"I do."

"You don't. I don't think you like Japan."

"Oh, here we go. I love Japan. I have always loved Japan. That's where we met, Sara. You're from Japan."

"That's what I mean." Sara said. Then she sank into petulant silence.

"And, what about Ceci?" she asked suddenly.

"What about her, Sara?" Gene said. "That's over, isn't it?"

"Maybe for you, callous man. My heart is broken."

Gene didn't bother to answer. He knew any defense was hopeless. So, wisely, he said nothing, and the silence deepened and festered—until Gray screamed.

Gray's howl tore through the station wagon. It was, in some ways, what we needed. It lodged like a high-voltage alien next to a pineapple on the collar of Gene's Hawaiian shirt. It appeared to drive high-decibel needles down into his spine. The fine brown hairs at the nape of Gene's neck seemed to crackle and rise. The backs of his ears turned red. The car lurched forward, picking up speed. Sara swiveled in the front seat to look back at us. Her black sunglasses were a Kato-like mask, her lips a bright crimson color. She looked like the Green Hornet's Japanese sidekick.

"You children are pushing it," she said.

Ignoring Sara, Gray screamed again. All eyes turned to the back of the station wagon. Gray had a bad temper. His face had turned a violent plum-purple. Flecks of white foam dotted his full, lower lip. He was shaking.

Less than a stranglehold away from Gray, Mimi cowered in the very back of the station wagon, her body pressed into the corner where Gray's wail had pinned her. Her black eyes, under the shiny, newly-cut fringe of her bangs, were full of her peril. On her lap was Gray's bible—a fat picture book thick with color plates depicting King Arthur, his knights, their jousts and wars. This was Gray's most valued possession. With me in the backseat, Samuel leaned back against the car door, an appreciative smile on his lips. He approved of all passionate outbursts.

Samuel had great charisma. Of all of us, Sam looked the least Japanese. He looked like Gene with his light brown hair; but the thick, dark lashes that fringed his eyes were like

Sara's. Samuel's handsome face and dazzling hazel eyes had earned him the name of "Mr. Hollywood" from flirty girls much older than he—older, even, than I. Samuel was Sara's favorite child, and Gray was his avid disciple. He wanted to be just like Sam.

Gene pulled the car off the road at the next available turnout. Mimi's crayons flew from the window ledges where Samuel and Gray had lined them up. They were peeled and by this time softening nicely in the Death Valley sun. A dust cloud billowed around us.

Gray was too angry to speak. Now that the car had stopped, we could all see the source of his fury. While the boys had stripped and lined up her crayons, five-year-old Mimi had entertained herself by covering the glossy pages of Gray's bible with the dervish-like doodles of a single green crayon. She had covered the white space. All the illustrations were now buried under the net of her scrawl.

This was not, by the way, an uncommon practice in our family. Each of us had spent time hiding behind the living room couch, filling the pages of the household library with art. The best fish Gray ever drew was in one of those books, as were Samuel's legions of rotund men in hats, and my much-praised series of pin-headed girls. We were our own biggest fans, and the drawings in Sara and Gene's favorite books were an accepted form of expression. Sara never seemed to mind. The pictures made her laugh, and they were all right with Gene, since they amused Sara. In fact, as Mimi sat quietly browsing Gray's book, I had been unable to resist slipping her the green crayon. I regretted it, of course, because it had upset Gray so badly. But in a way, Gray's outburst was a huge relief. Nothing was worse than Sara and Gene's crabby silence.

Gene slammed out of the car and walked along the road shoulder, away from us.

While he stood there at the roadside, looking into the culvert, probably wondering how his life had turned into a child-choked fiasco, Sara invited Gray up into the front seat with her. "He'll just have to get over it," Sara said, looking out the front windshield at Gene. "Gray, you come up here. You must forgive Mimi; she's your little sister. I'm sure she's sorry."

Gray climbed over the seat backs and took a seat next to Sara. That's what he wanted anyway. He wanted to sit in the front between Sara and Gene. He wanted Sara to cover his face with kisses, leaving lipstick marks all over his forehead and cheeks. Samuel's eyes sparkled as he watched Gray wriggle onto the seat next to Sara. Samuel had been there, too, a few short years before—under Sara's protective arm. It seemed to make both boys a little drunk.

Sara had that effect on everyone. She wiped the tears from Gray's face with a scented and packaged towelette that she kept in her purse for moments like this one. Her fingernails, like her lips, were bright red. Her thick, straight, dark hair tented them both. People said that I looked like Sara, but I didn't believe them. Her person was a combination of planes and angles in graceful relationship. My body had lately decided to move in lumpish directions. It made me think of the summer when I found tadpoles in the stream near our house. They were tiny, dark commas darting around in the cloudy water. I carried them home in an old coffee can, and Sara provided a fishbowl to raise them in. I was horrified by their growth. Soon they filled the fishbowl. They turned from black to an ugly mud-gray. Their bellies bulged. Squat legs began to protrude from their once-smooth sides. Their tails thickened, rotted, and eventually fell off. They ate their own tails, and they ate one another. I couldn't feed them enough. They'd turned into hideous monsters.

They swam sluggishly about in the water, preparing to turn into frogs. I couldn't stand looking at them. Sara said it was only a phase. I asked Gene what he thought.

"Well, Ellen," he said, "I agree with you. They really are ugly. What I would do is throw them back into that stream."

I told Gene that I thought he was right. So, Gene and I returned to the stream with the fishbowl, and I poured the tadpoles back into the water they'd come from.

I couldn't help wondering, feeling as awkward and unattractive as I did that spring, if Gene didn't want to take me and throw me back into the water, too.

Meanwhile, with Gray in the front seat with Sara and the danger removed, Mimi returned to perfect bliss in her private Siberia in the back of the station wagon. All the parts of her Giant Cootie game were spread out around her, along with four dirty potatoes stabbed with noses and eyes. There was gum on her blanket and crayola all over her clothes.

We were all wondering what Gene was going to do. After some minutes, he came back to the car.

"Climb back to the rear, Gray," he said, thumb pointing over his shoulder toward the back of the station wagon. Sara gave Gray a meaningful pat. Gray climbed back over the seat. Gene started the car up, and we were again on our way.

"Gene, can we go to the Twenty Mule Team Canyon?" I asked, still reading from the book on my lap, thinking we were all ready for a serious destination. "Can we go to Zabriskie Point?"

"Yeah," said Gene. "Good idea, Ellen. Sara, what do you think?" he asked warily.

"Sounds fine," Sara said tersely.

"Done," Gene resolved, following Highway 190 past Furnace Creek Ranch, west toward Death Valley Junction.

Twenty Mule Team Canyon was nothing but a narrow road winding through bare gray hills lined with tufts of white fuzz.

"That's the borax," Gene said.

"Borax crystals," I corrected, wishing a wagon with a twenty-mule team would come rushing by, block our way, and charge the air with excitement. It was terribly hot in the car. Mimi said she was going to throw up.

"We'll get out and walk at Zabriskie Point," Gene told us. "You kids can have sodas. I need a beer."

At Zabriskie Point, we piled out of the car, got our drinks and ran to the edge of the lookout. Beneath us the badlands stretched in fold after fold of pinched yellow earth. Sara made us all pose for a photo—four dusty, sweat-soaked, part-Asian kids, grinning into the camera.

I liked looking out over the badlands, the chemical-loaded plateau of hills that rose and fell in wave after wave of packed earth like a lifeless sea reaching out toward the horizon. It was quiet, except for our occasional squeals. I could almost hear the earth humming.

"I want to stay here," I whispered.

I looked over at Gene. He was drinking a beer and taking long, slow drags from a cigarette. Sara was fussing with Mimi and the boys, wiping their faces, making them tuck in their shirts.

"Japan," I thought miserably. "Japan. Who wants to go to Japan?" My problem was that no place seemed to be the right place for me. Japan was probably as bad as anywhere else—maybe worse. I just didn't fit in. Even in Sara's photos my presence seemed like an error. I looked longingly down into the soundless ochre maze.

"The badlands," I murmured to myself. "I want to live in the badlands."

Sara and Gene were too concerned with significant details to notice any of this.

Our journey ended, early, in San Diego. San Diego was full of palm trees, beaches, and bungalows that, in turn, were full of mothers with strollers full of whey-faced, sour-stomached, colicky babies. We arrived in San Diego ahead of Gene's schedule. It had been a pretty rough trip, and he was glad to be calling it quits.

In San Diego we stayed for a while in a beach house on Mission Bay that belonged to Gene's sister's boyfriend. It had a patio and a small, fenced yard that ended right on the sand. We looked like we didn't belong on that beach. With the exception of Gene and Samuel, we looked like Japanese spies. Gene made matters worse by being oblivious to this and spending most of his time in the yard. He was recovering from the trip. He lounged around in his swim trunks and bright Hawaiian shirts drinking scotch on the rocks and flirting with the girls on the opposite side of the fence. His eyes were bloodshot from his dips in the bay. His nose was flamingo-pink. Sometimes he plunked around conspicuously on a ukulele, in case anyone had missed the bright shirts and the sunburn. Next to him, sipping mixed drinks on a chaise longue, Sara sat, cool and pallid, hidden under a sunbonnet and dark glasses. Neither of them seemed aware of how peculiar they looked. They were in their own world, and they liked it.

In the meantime, Samuel, Mimi, and Gray were destroying the boyfriend's house. Their fingerprints covered the sliding glass doors, their footprints covered the chalk-colored carpets. Mimi managed to drop a piece of grape jelly sandwich behind one of the chairs, but this wasn't discovered until long trails of ants were traced to the well-hidden tidbit. Sand found its way into the beds and their artwork into the books. I wasn't surprised when we were thrown out, Gene's sister, Lillie, along with us. She moved back in with some friends, and we moved to a motel on the other side of the highway. Compared to the beach, we'd moved to a very colorful neighborhood. The motel had a pool. It was full of Mexican families. Sara hated the place. Gene sat in the sun and got redder.

Finally Sara said, "Enough is enough. Are we going or aren't we?"

She made Gene change the tickets, and the next thing we knew, we were boarding the flight for Japan.

I was glad to be leaving the stuffy, moist warmth of the California coast, but it was almost as though I'd outgrown the plane. Because Gene's job took him all over the world, we were used to traveling by plane. I usually enjoy airplane journeys. This time it was different. Mimi, Samuel, and Gray marched back and forth down the aisles on constant forays and trips to the restrooms as I had once done, while I sat stuck to my seat, as though trapped, between my fold-out tray and the fat knees of the enormous adult sitting next to me. At one point, I went to the restroom, but the lock on the door was a new kind and I couldn't figure out how to work it. I was too proud to ask for help, so I left the restroom unlocked when I used it. There I was, sitting on the toilet, with my shorts down around my knees, when the door was opened by a tall man in a uniform—the pilot. He filled the doorway. He just stood there with a dopey smile on his face.

"Oh, I'm sorry," he said, and hastily retreated. He bumped his head on top of the doorway. He, too, had to struggle with the door. If I had been younger, it wouldn't have bothered me, but at ten years old, I was mortified. I slinked back to my seat and did not move for the rest of the flight. I couldn't even look at the stewardesses.

"I walked in on a kid using the lavatory," I imagined the pilot telling them. "There she is. That girl, over there."

Feeling sorry for myself, I narrowly eyed the fat man sitting next to me. Part of his body hung over the partition between us, like a muffin rising over its tin. His arm kept banging against mine. I wanted to punch it back into place.

"Pretty small seats," he said amiably. I gave him a sour look and turned to the window. I stared out. I slept. When I awoke, listless and groggy, it was to a startling sight. The sky had become an incredible orange color, as if someone had lit it on fire. Ahead of us loomed a great wall of darkness. We were moving through sunset into the night. We were close to Japan. I perched on the edge of my seat, face pressed to the window, as far away as I could get from the fat man and his arm. The wall of darkness loomed closer and closer. Then we punctured it. The plane pierced the curtain like a needle moving through velvet, and the world around us went black. We traveled for what seemed like a very short, silent time in that void. Then the "fasten your seat belt" signs went on. The stewardesses announced our arrival and the airplane set down in Japan. When we disembarked, the pilot stood at the door. The adults shuffled past with farewells, the children with ice-cream-cone grins. I tried to sneak by.

"Hello, again. Nice flight?" he asked jauntily and winked, as if we shared some hilarious secret.

I wanted to kick him in the shins and run, but I was in a slow-moving queue. Instead, I glowered at him from under my bangs with the fiercest face I could muster until I was safely past.

Of course, I forgot all about this when we stepped into the Tokyo airport, into that sea of similar-seeming ivory faces. It was startling. They all looked a little like Sara. Gene, who is five feet eleven inches tall, towered over the crowd. The din in the airport was loud and intrusive, the smells diff-erent, the people small and hurried, and I couldn't understand a word they said.

Almost at once, Sara herded us into two taxis. Mimi and I sat with her in one; Gene took the boys in another. We hurled through crowded night-lit streets swimming in neon. Our driver had rolled his front window down. He blew soft clouds of cigarette smoke out into the night. Waves of moisture-heavy air, freighted with strange combinations of sounds and aromas rushed back at us. Traffic noise, broken wisps of a high-pitched, nasal singing, the smell of grilled fish, of stale beer, of gar-denias wafted in from the dark carnival roiling outside the cabs. Then, the streets became quieter, less peopled. The taxis shrieked to a stop.

A couple of stony guardians, lion-like creatures with wide-opened jaws crouching on the balustrades of a wall of shallow steps, marked the approach to a Japanese hotel. Samuel and Gray swarmed them at once, caressing the blunt-snouted faces. Mimi inched closer to Sara, hand tightening around Sara's fingertips. Two porters dressed in white materialized like wraiths, descended the steps and bowed, their white-gloved hands dipping into the trunks of the cabs and retrieving our luggage. In single file—Gene leading, Mimi and Sara in the rear, the porters bobbing ahead like a pair of lanterns—we climbed the stairs and followed a flagstone trail through a wall of dark pines and over a small bridge. Our reflections in the waters below were threaded with the slow glide of fish the color of silver and flame.

More cedars and pines flanked the lobby entrance, only these had been trimmed into curious shapes. The night air was sharp with the clean scent of their needles. I was shocked by the order, the absence of clutter, and the silence. We children were loud without saying a word, and I wished that our clothes all matched or that we were all the same size.

"Hey, Gray, Gray, this is a hotel," I heard Samuel whisper excitedly.

The name of the hotel was the Daimyô. It was huge and constructed mainly of wood and stone that was cracked and furred with moss. The manager, a thin, dark-suited man, greeted us in the lobby.

"Welcome," he said, head bowed slightly, eyes closed. "Please, come this way."

He whistled the "s's" and made all the "l's" sound like "r's." We queued in behind him like ducklings and followed him to a part of the hotel that looked very different from the rest.

"Gomenasai—so, sorry," he said to Sara, "your honorable mother specified Japanese-style rooms. Please, I hope you find this one acceptable."

I heard a communal gasp as he slid open the door. I poked my head in through the opening. The room before us was so simple. The floor, which was raised and had to be stepped up onto, was divided into black-bordered 6 foot by 3 foot rectangles of tightly woven straw-colored tatami. A low black lacquer table, surrounded by flat zabuton pillows of saffron-colored silk, sat at its center. Upon this table, a black vase from which white orchids, dried lotus pods, and curly green willow towered, dominated the space. A small white card was propped next to the vase.

"Please. Dozo," the manager said gesturing up toward the room. "The Daimyô welcomes you."

"It's lovely," Sara said softly.

The manager smiled, closed his eyes and nodded. He seemed quite pleased with himself.

Beyond this room was another very small one. Lacquer lattice-work doors with panes of rice paper had been left ajar, and we could see the deep purple and mustard colors of heavy silk futons upon which to sleep.

Six people in that room would be a tight fit.

"We are all to sleep here?" Sara asked carefully.

"Oh, I'm very sorry," the manager answered, somewhat embarrassed. "Your honorable mother clearly specified that the children should have their own room."

"Oh," said Sara trying to mask her concern. "Oh, I see."

I watched a wide grin spread irrepressibly over Gene's face.

Mimi, Gray, Samuel, and I were put into a different room, a children's dormitory. But we were the only children in it. Perhaps it had been a ballroom once or a room for billeting troops in the Second World War. It was long, like a wide hall, with a spacious red-carpeted walkway down the center. A draft seemed to sing through it. Against each of the two longer walls was a row of narrow metal beds with only a few feet between each of them. A hundred people could have slept in that room. It looked like a hospital.

But the strangest part of the room was its guardians. It was flanked on two sides by eight carved wooden statues, each nearly fourteen feet high. Along one wall loomed four demons, or oni, and on the other four powerful kami, or gods. The gods were carved in yellow wood that gleamed like ivory, the demons in dark red wood. Some had horns and strange top knots. Some were obese. They all had dramatic faces, pop-eyes and grimaces that terrified Mimi. She wrapped her thin arms and legs around Sara and refused to let go.

"Look, Mimi," Sara said, unwinding the spidery limbs of her youngest child like a woman removing a stole. "There are four oni and four kami. Four demons. Four gods. It's balanced. They'll use up all their strength fighting each other and you children will be perfectly safe."

That seemed to satisfy Mimi, who let go of Sara. She hugged her blanket instead. Since the gods were just as scary as the demons, we chose beds on the demon side of the room. Samuel and Gray dealt with their fear by climbing the statues. Gray tweaked the long nose of a tengu, or goblin. It had round eyes and nails like a tiger's claws. Samuel crawled into and reclined on the lap of a beautiful woman entwined with a sea serpent. Sara told us her name was Bentan. She was the goddess of art. The sea serpent's mouth was wide open. It looked like it was going to devour the goddess, and Samuel, enthroned in her lap, looked like he'd be part of the meal.

One of the gods carried a big fish called a tai. Another held a hammer in one hand and a bulging sack in the other. He straddled two rice bales. Mimi was eye-level with the lifelike batallion of rats that were savagely attacking the rice bales. My favorite deity, Fukurokuju, was a squat-statured, pin-headed figure. A crane or a heron tucked under his arm reached up with its long neck and beak to pick at his beard.

"Hey, Ellen, that one looks like one of your drawings," Gray observed from under the tengu's nose.

I shrugged, suddenly very unhappy about having to sleep in the same room as Samuel, Mimi, and Gray. "Yes, I guess so," I said.

When they tired of crawling about on the statues, they started a game that consisted of jumping from one bed to the next without letting their feet touch the floor. Mimi, always unable to resist their games, soon joined them. They wore themselves out. By dinnertime they were exhausted.

Dinner was a late meal and a strange one—our first with chopsticks. The restaurant Gene selected was in the hotel. It offered Japanese and western cuisines, but Gray's chicken sandwich tasted like fish. Mimi toyed with the chopsticks, purposefully dropping little bits of slippery red and yellow Japanese pickles that she had no intention of eating on her lap in the hope that Sara would notice. Samuel made sucking sounds with his soup, slurping up buckwheat noodles from the rich, pork-filled broth in imitation of a man eating noodles a few tables away. Sara tried to ignore us. Gene kept ordering bite-sized morsels of rice and raw fish and thumb-sized cups of rice wine. I figured it would be a long dinner. It would take lots of these to fill Gene up. He was blissfully happy with his sushi and sake.

In spite of Sara's protests to the contrary, Gene loved Japan. He was probably also pleased that he would have Sara all to himself, a rarity considering their retinue of dependents. So, we spent our first night in Japan, separated from Sara and Gene, lost in nightmares induced by our unusual food, in the shadow of grimacing demons, while across the room, the equally frightening gods kept watch over our slumbers.

The morning was painful—awkward and bright. Sara had, with little foresight, neglected to pack anything but our play clothes, the ones we'd been traipsing around Montana and Wyoming in all summer long. These looked decidedly out of place in our new, pin-neat environment. We were going to meet Grandmother that day. Sara and Gene regarded us closely.

"Oh, they look all right," Gene said, trying to forestall the inevitable.

"I suppose," Sara agreed reluctantly. "Well, at least they look healthy and happy."

I noticed that she seemed to be counting the scabs on Mimi's skinny brown legs. I thought the danger was over. We appeared to have passed their inspection. Then Sara spoiled it.

"But what about Ellen?" she asked.

"What about her?" Gene responded warily.

"Well, Gene, don't you think Ellen should be wearing a dress?"

Gene's look of shock must have mirrored my own.

"We have time," Sara sang out cheerfully. "I'll take Ellen shopping in the Ginza. We'll be back in no time."

The Ginza, in Tokyo, is a district packed with office buildings, banks, museums, and high-rise department stores. The streets teemed with workers and shoppers, with women in kimonos and cute summer suits, with men in white shirtsleeves and others in dark suits and ties. They moved like a tide up sidewalks, across streets. Heat undulated upward in sweltering waves from the asphalt and concrete. It bounced off the glass and steel faces of the business towers that rose up around us. On the seventh floor of the Matsuzakaya Department Store, Sara found the odious dress. It had a too-high waist and a poofy skirt. It was made of egg-colored piqué. I don't know why Sara chose it, except that she was in a hurry, and I was being particularly uncooperative. The salesgirl was her fawning accomplice. I looked at myself in the mirror of that Japanese department store with the pesty clerk hovering over me, and I was appalled.

"I look like a larva," I said.

"Hardly," said Sara, loosening my hair. She purchased the dress.

"Well, Ellen," Gene remarked upon our return, "you certainly look different." He did not seem too pleased with the effect.

Samuel, Mimi, and Gray snickered unsympathetically. I was going to meet Grandmother like that, like a piqué-swathed grub. It was as I had feared. I ate my lunch in combative silence.

Grandmother did not seem to be dying to me. That was, I decided, a lie. She lived in a small house in the Rappongi district of Tokyo. Sara said that she was living on interest, and it seemed by the way she said it that this was a very good thing to do. We took two cabs to her house. Grandmother dressed like a man in a silk shirt and slacks. She wore slippers. She spoke only Japanese, except to Gene, whom she seemed to like a lot. I could tell that she was not at all impressed by my dress and shared my disgust, so I went to a lot of trouble not to be too obtrusive so as not to irritate her. Not that it mattered; she seemed to take very little notice of any of us.

Her maid, on the other hand, wore traditional Japanese dress—a kimono and white socks called tabi. She thought Samuel and Gray were incredibly cute and kept smiling at them and nodding her head in a funny way. Then, catching Grandmother's eye for some sort of approval, she stood up and padded out of the room. She returned in moments with a beautiful tasseled box with Japanese writing on it. She lifted the lid and inside were what any child would recognize as cookies, only these had intricately carved surfaces and were raised and filled.

"Dozo," she nodded, smiling, holding the box toward my brothers. Their quick hands darted into the crinkly paper, retrieving a cookie each.

"Dozo," she said to Mimi and me.

We, too, helped ourselves to the beautiful cookies.

I bit gingerly into mine, not wanting to crush the artfully sculpted design all at once, expecting the comforting taste that I thought was universal. I looked immediately at Samuel and Gray who had both taken enormous bites, their smiles frozen on clenched jaws, while the maid nodded and smiled, the sickening taste of sweet bean paste filling their mouths. That we got through that first bite was a testament to Sara's rigorous training, though I watched Gray's mouth open wide twice, lined with red bean, until Sara's cold stare made him close it.

Grandmother observed this with a thin, disinterested gaze, her face as smoothly immobile as wax. Then she made a gesture, not missed by the maid, who caught it, and obeyed. Rising hypnotically, she moved with trancelike certainty toward and out of the sliding door. The silk of her kimono rustled around her slippered, white-socked feet. Grandmother rose, too, the front creases of her trousers straightening as she stood, stopping just short of her velvet-slippered feet. She, too, disappeared into another room like the one we were in—boxes within boxes—the same precise squares of tatami, the same carefully divided, palely-printed rice-paper panes. The maid returned with rice wine on a red lacquer tray and placed it on the low black table before Sara and Gene. My parents sat in silence, sipping their sake. Sara's face bore a contemplative expression, one that neither I nor any of her other three indefatigable children had ever seen, and seeing it now, made me nervous.

On the other side of the room, Samuel, Mimi, and Gray were fidgeting, preparing to fight if the enforced immobility were to continue. Casually untangling herself from their conspiratorial knot, Mimi rose languidly and began shuffling around, her feet like all of ours, pressed into slippered sedation. Like a careless dragonfly, she moved from object to object, touching everything—the scrolls that hung on the grass-cloth covered walls, the lean flower arrangements, the dark bronzes. I did not need to hold them to know that her hands were still sticky with the dark paste from those cookies and that she left her spoor here and there where she touched, as surely as a bee leaves pollen.

Unlike Mimi, Samuel and Gray were unable to move from place to place without tumbling over someone, and were squirming, their hazel eyes dancing, goaded to a feverish pitch by her impish progress around the room. They poked each other in the ribs. They hammerlocked one another's heads and communicated in these movements, their plan for her arrest.

"Saru-domo yo sotode asobi-nasai. Monkeys play outside." Grandmother's statement entered the room before her.

She had walked in carrying a large, crocodile-skin portfolio. It looked very old. She opened it out on the low table before my parents. It was full of stacks of documents, some wrapped around with purple cord. All were covered with neat vertical lines of spidery scratches that looked a little like Sara's letters. I moved closer to see what they were, but the writing that crept down the page looked like barbed wire, an incomprehensible fence that I couldn't possibly climb.

"There are several deeds here," Sara explained to Gene, "two for Tokyo properties and one for the house on Lake

Towada; they're the homes that Mama built after the war. There's a will, the genealogy, Mama's bank documents, and all of my papers." Sara shuffled carefully through the yellowed stacks.

"Mama," she exclaimed suddenly, "you bought back Akishima!"

"Yes," Grandmother said simply. "Our ancestral home. Our property. But, it will go, of course, to my younger brothers, to your uncles after my death." She turned to Gene. "But, you see, Gene, even without Akishima, Sara will be a very rich woman after I die."

"That isn't what matters," Gene said quickly. "Love matters."

"Love means nothing," Grandmother responded keenly. "Duty matters. Family matters. Why wander?" she continued. "It's foolish. Sara has so much to offer."

I found Sara's agitation, the small red blotch on each of her cheeks, disturbing. Grandmother sat back on her heels, her expressionless gaze fixed on Gene. Gene stared down at the table as if trying to read the black lacquer surface. Samuel and Gray were kicking one another, disintegrating under the extremity of their boredom. Mimi was circling around them, her little foot, in an adult slipper, touching one boy's leg, then another, taunting and springing away.

Sara looked up absently.

"Children, go play outside."

She addressed us as a single body. I winced. Was she talking to me? Certainly not in the dress. I looked around self-consciously, frustrated by my own uncertainty. Samuel,

Mimi, and Gray were already moving toward the door. I looked to Sara for some separate message as to exactly what I should do. She and Grandmother were talking again.

"But, Mama, how could you possibly purchase . . . ?"

"Piece by piece, at great personal loss," Grandmother snapped. "They should never have lost it. It's our legacy. Men can be fools.

"As for your family," she continued, addressing Gene, "you will never have to worry about money. But that will be after I die."

Gene was listening intently. The maid sat calmly in attendance.

"And I will be gone soon enough," she added. "But for now, this child . . ." Grandmother looked at me sharply. "You have two fine sons," she said firmly, "but this oldest girl—my granddaughter . . ." she began. Then, she switched to Japanese like a train jumping tracks. I heard my name mentioned once, twice in my grandmother's forceful tones. Sara's voice sounded placating. She seemed embarrassed. Gene looked nervous. Then they both looked at me. It was clear that they didn't want me to hear, and I knew that my grandmother had nothing good to say about me. And I certainly couldn't blame her. I rose stiffly then, and walked with as much dignity as I could manage out of the room, out of the house.

I exited through the genkan, a small anteroom where colorful slippers waited in rows, heel-to-heel with outdoor boots and shoes, umbrellas, a few gardening tools, and wide-brimmed straw hats. The red leaves of a Japanese maple had settled untidily on the gravel and flagstones. They looked like small, bloody handprints. I stopped in the garden. It was empty. Samuel, Mimi, and Gray were already out on the street, their voices rising and falling, three little strays trotting out into the maze of shops and restaurants that cluttered the neighborhood.

"You'd better put your shoes on."

"Listen, I can speak Japanese: 'ano-nê, ano kazu.'"

"That doesn't sound right."

"Look at what Gene gave me. It's yen."

"Hey, that's money."

"Let's go to the store."

"Can I buy some paper?"

"Yeah, but you have to wear those slippers to the store."

"Okay."

"And you have to walk up to someone and say 'Ano-nê.'"

"I will. Okay"

"Ano-nê."

"Ano-nê."

"Ano-nê."

Three voices, laughter drifting back toward me.

I wanted to be with them, careless and unencumbered. But I had been singled out, isolated like a worm in my embarrassing cocoon of piqué. Unable to advance or retreat, I waited clumsily on the path, stuck in the garden, trapped in that no-man's land between Grandmother's house and the Tokyo street.

3

yurei yashiki |
ghost house

My family took its leave of Grandmother with the same con-
fusion with which we did everything. Sara and Gene smiled
wanly, apologetic for the mad scramble of children collecting
their things. Samuel, Mimi, and Gray had a way of accumu-
lating objects—rocks, old junk, street dust—whatever happened to be in their vicinity. Separation from their
surroundings was always an arduous process.

"Leave that here, that's your grandmother's," Sara snapped
at Mimi, who had just pocketed a handful of nuts and a tiny
ceramic tortoise.

"Oh, sorry," Mimi said perfunctorily. She opened her hand
and the loosened booty rolled noisily in all directions over the
lacquer surface of Grandmother's table. Gray and Samuel gathered their coats. Part of a cookie that had found its way into one
of their pockets, was stepped on and ground into the tatami.
The neat rows of slippers that lined the genkan doorway had
deteriorated into a jumble. They were no longer properly

mated, but paired, instead, with this gardening tool or that half-opened umbrella. Mimi could not find both of her socks. The one she did find was a small, grayish ball. Sara took it from her with an admonishing look and slid it quickly into her purse. By the time the children were lined up at the genkan door to kiss Grandmother good-bye, Gene had started to scowl. Sara looked worried. Grandmother and her maid, scandalized by the chaos, remained coolly aloof. Each child marched up as Sara had instructed and dutifully kissed the cheek that Grandmother proffered. I waited politely until the others were done. Then I walked up to Grandmother to give her what I thought was a granddaughterly kiss. She drew back, surprised. She seemed more offended than pleased. The maid's brows raised to form a small teepee of chagrin.

"Oh, no, dear," Sara whispered, "You will be staying with Grandma."

I couldn't believe what I'd heard. I turned to Mimi, Samuel, and Gray. They were quarreling over some rub-on tattoos that they'd bought at a Japanese store. Gene was watching them glumly, probably thinking of Tokyo traffic or dinner reservations. He wanted to leave.

"Oh," I responded, a knot, like paste, in my throat. "Oh. Well, I guess I'll see you tomorrow."

"You'll have a wonderful time," Sara said, smiling and hugging me falsely. Sara knew that this was far from the truth. I felt I had been betrayed.

"Good-bye, Ellen," Gene added, kissing me on the forehead right through my bangs.

"'Bye," I mumbled. I stepped back up to the porch with Grandmother and her maid to watch my parents battle their way down the slender garden path with their children, as if herding three furious little pygmies through high and impassable brush.

At first I was angry. I thought of Samuel, Mimi, and Gray in the dark, statued ballroom. I imagined them exploring the recesses of the hotel. I pictured Sara and Gene suffering through another dinner with them, alert to the possible catastrophes, dismayed by the inadequate table manners of their children and exhausted by their endless exuberance. Then all my things arrived by messenger from the hotel, and I realized with a pang that I would not be going back to them the next morning. I watched with horror as the maid expertly unpacked my few travel clothes from my suitcase and placed them in the drawers of a cherry wood dresser in one of the bedrooms. She moved expertly. Within minutes, my clothes vanished into that deceptively blank facade and the suitcase disappeared. My mouth grew dryer as she pushed each of the small drawers shut. She looked at me cheerily, brisk as a nurse opening sickroom curtains, her mind on other things. It was clear by her manner that she had no idea as to the depth of my despair.

"I reeve you," she attempted, in English, with a very deep bow.

I nodded unable to speak. And I was left alone.

There is a great deal of privacy in a Japanese house. Nothing is hidden, except thoughts and feelings. But of these, nothing is seen. I moved awkwardly through the rooms of my grandmother's house feeling graceless and out of place. I wandered into the kitchen. Three bottles of milk sat on the counter. I tore off the red metal caps and sniffed at the milk in the bottles to see if it, at least, was familiar. The milk smelled old and faintly perfumed, like old flower petals, and for some reason that made me sad. There were bamboo steamers full of long noodles that looked like cellophane worms. Glass pots full of sour-smelling pickles and hairy, white radish mounds sat next to bowls in which cream-colored, flower-shaped disks and turnip-like slices riddled with holes were suspended. Nothing looked very familiar.

I tiptoed into Grandmother's bedroom, the largest room in the house. Gold and silver-framed photographs of suited and uniformed men, of dancers, actresses, pretty girls and boys, crowded her mahogany dresser. On the dressing table, a dozen lacquered, lidded pots were neatly arranged. I peered into them, hoping to find secrets, clues and answers written in English, something that explained who my grandmother really was, and why I'd been left with her. They held nothing but lead-white powders and dusty rouges. Colorful pieces of silk covered some of the furniture surfaces. There was nothing else in the room except silk pillows, futons, and six metal-lined tea chests. I opened one. It was full of beautiful clothes —dresses in velvet, satin, and chiffon that smelled curiously of a mixture of mothballs and the dark aroma of tea.

From some of the photographs on Grandmother's dresser, Sara stared, a puny, severe child with straight dark hair and eyes as black as two olives, a giant taffeta bow sticking up from the top of her head. She looked scared and lonely with the trappings of wealth all around her. In one early photo, she hugged a pair of ice skates, in another, a fluffy white dog. In a few of the later snapshots, she smiled widely, older and aggressive, her long hair brushed back, her almond-shaped eyes still shiny and dark. In other photos, men in linen suits and ties and women in broad-brimmed hats, on picnics or posing by automobiles, grinned at the camera. Grandmother, in a waistcoat and tie, her dark hair bobbed and waved, leaned with her friends against a churchyard wall or dipped dramatically on a stage with a fringed Spanish shawl draped around her shoulders.

I sat back on the futons and stared at the photos through half-closed eyes. I flipped through a black photo album that I'd found in one of the tea chests. The names of the people, the places and dates, were written underneath each picture, in English. The white crayon captions made the pages look like a boneyard. Sara had already introduced us to some of the ghosts—to Aunt Sally, the missionary, and to the tragic twins, Katsuko and Karl. Karl died of leukemia at twelve. Katsuko died a year later of the same disease. Sara had shared all of these stories. She told us about China, where she was raised. She told us about fires and wars. Sara did not edit her stories for children. I wished she hadn't told us as much as she had. She had clouded our world with the dark history of her family, with stories of death, flights, and lovers. Canton. Tiger Mountain. Algiers. Bombay. Footless beggars in Shanghai.

Houses on fire. A man without a head running beside her. Furs traded for cabbages.

In the bedroom that I had been given, the maid had left a terry cloth kimono striped in pale pink and lavender that I think was Grandmother's, and a large white bath towel. She returned to the room to fetch me, smiling, her teeth wet and shiny as pearls. She nodded, the way she had nodded at Samuel and Gray and indicated by gestures that I was to put on the kimono. I was certain the robe and a towel meant a bath. I followed her, out of the house, clomping along in geta, the awkward wooden clogs she'd given me to wear. We crossed the small patio at the back of the house. We came to a wooden building. It looked like a large dollhouse. It was walled on one side by sliding shoji doors, panels framing opaque panes of milky white glass.

"Dozo," the maid said, smiling. She moved politely aside.

I stepped out of the geta and up to the raised entrance. The door slid open easily. Hot steam rushed through the doorway to greet me.

"Dozo," the maid said again.

I nodded, and stooping a little and continuing to bob my head, backed my way in. Sliding the door shut, I sighed. All of my misery surfaced. Everything was too strange. It was unbearable. I took a deep gulp of the comforting steam. I was ready, almost, to cry.

Behind me I heard the quick fall of water, the scrape of a wooden stool, and a voice.

"Koko-ni osuwari."

I wheeled, startled, to see Grandmother standing, pale as marble, a glistening apparition in a halo of steam. Her gray hair was pulled up in a hard, tight bun on top of her head. She was naked. Lanky and thin, the sheen of her whiteness was like death. A faint triangle shadowed the joint of her lower limbs. Her face, implacable, seemed carved out of stone. In her right hand she held a big wooden dipper. A look of impatience moved quickly across her face.

I stood, also, as though I were frozen, shrouded in curling steam, the kimono still wrapped about me. I did not know quite what to do. Grandmother motioned toward the blue-tiled wall where a couple of empty hooks jutted. I looked sadly down at my pink and lavender robe. With the glum resolution of one condemned, I walked to the wall, took it off, and hung it on the hook, my fingers lingering over its folds.

Grandmother regarded me critically. She handed me the dipper.

In the corner of the room was a round wooden tub, full of water, with a fire burning under it—the source of the steam. It looked like a cannibal's stewpot.

"Oyu otoringisai," Grandmother said, demonstrating how to "scoop the water out of the hot tub" and "pour it over you." I did as her gesturing indicated, taking a large dipperful of water and pouring it over my body, afraid to make a mistake. It was scalding. I squeezed my eyes shut, trying hard not to flinch.

"Koyatte, yoku karada yusugu-no desu-yo."

I watched as she pantomimed washing and rinsing and pointed me toward the tub. She handed me a tiny white cake of soap and turned, bending to pick up her own, her lean buttocks pointing toward me. Standing outside the tub, she began to wash herself carefully, caressingly, with the rectangle of soap, her hands sliding along her limbs, slipping down her neck, around her thin breasts. She took a handful of rock salt from a ceramic crock and rubbed it into her shins, her calves, and her thighs, until her lower extremities, buttocks to toes, were streaked a furious red. All of this she did with complete disregard of my close observation. I played with the white cake of soap and rubbed it haphazardly here and there; my focus entirely on Grandmother. She punctuated every procedure with a dipperful of the scalding water. Her head flung back, I watched her inhale deeply and groan, her eyes half shut, unaware of me, unconcerned with my child-body, my self-consciousness, and my surprise.

My body looked nothing like hers. It was not porcelain-white. It was nut-brown from days in Montana and Wyoming, from days in the desert. I didn't have breasts, just two pink buttons on a flat chest that was beginning to puff out in a couple of hump-shaped mounds. I tried not to pay much attention to them. Once, years ago, my friend Alison and I had painted our nipples a flashing Mercurochrome orange, using what we'd found in the medicine cabinet. The Mercurochrome bled through our blouses, making two round stains on the laundered white of our chests. Our mothers were scandalized. They separated us. We could not play together for weeks. I realized, then, that nipples were off-limits. It really was best to ignore them.

Grandmother did not seem to regard things in this manner. She climbed the steps up to the tub, stepped over the rim, and immersed herself in the water. She closed her eyes. The sweat beaded up like dew on her upper lip, on her brow. Her face flushed rosy under the steel gray helmet of her tightly-combed hair. She seemed to rest that way for a long time. Every so often a purr-like groan would rumble deep in her throat. Fascinated, I now stared blatantly, having completely forgotten my dwindling bar of soap and my idle dabbing of this spot and that.

Climbing finally from the tub, she tossed a comment over her shoulder, offhandedly, in Japanese, "Hayaku shinasai." "Hurry up, child, or you will dry out," or something like that. She dressed quickly and left.

I was alone with the hot tub. I climbed into it, trying to imitate her, wanting to feel as she felt. I threw back my head and inhaled. It was hot. I thought of the giant king crabs that Gene had brought home one winter, how they bobbed around blushing crimson in a large cooking pot. We had cracked open the bodies with hammers, pulling and sucking the sweet white meat from the legs. I felt like one of those crabs. My body floated beneath me like an alien thing. It was turning bright red. I was getting so hot, I thought that I was going to explode. I was dizzy and becoming confused. *I'm going to be cooked,* I worried.

That scared me. I scrambled clumsily from the tub. I felt like crying again. The terry towel was horribly harsh on my flesh. It felt rough as sandpaper. All I could think of was how much I wanted to go home. I wanted everything to go back to normal. I thought of the red-haired woman, of my comment to Sara. That red-haired woman was the reason for this. She must have been an oni. I wished I had never spoken of her.

I put on the robe and stepped from the bathhouse. I nearly twisted my ankle trying to slip my feet into the geta. It was dark and quiet outside. Overhead, the sky was studded with stars. The night air was cool. The high bamboo-lined fence of Grandmother's garden screened out the city noise. I heard none of the Rappongi Street traffic. But I could hear Katan's tremulous whine and the repetitive liin-liin-liin of the bell-crickets suspended in their small bamboo cages up under the eaves and on Grandmother's windowsill. I could also hear television sounds drifting from the open window of an apartment next door. The suggestion of voices seemed to become entangled above me in the bamboo's dagger-like leaves. Japanese words and phrases, half-formed and unintelligible, wrestled overhead in the foliage, trying to reach me. Images from the black pages of Grandmother's photo albums filled my mind. I made Chinese eyes, pulling up on the corners of my eyelids and threw back my head to look at the stars. They swam in a blurry twinkle, shivered and slid like sprites of light. They looked strange, as strange as the world I was trapped in. Their weird stretches and shifts made me giddy. I felt a box open inside me. The sides flapped down and the bottom fell out. Everything became silent and empty. I rocked back under the shock. I felt raw, exposed and full of a horrible grief or loss. I waited, breath held, for something to happen. Nothing. The night air became suddenly bitter and painful, harsh like the rough terry towels. I walked very quickly back to the house.

Grandmother was waiting for me, seated in a kimono of red and green silk, at the black ozen table. In my bedroom, the futons that were to be my bed were already rolled out on the floor. A girl's silk kimono covered with brilliant fuchsias and tremendous aqua fans was spread upon them. The maid dressed me, first rubbing me hard with more terry cloth towels, then wrapping me into a thin red under-kimono, belting it and arranging a strip of silk over the collar before covering it with another kimono—one made of heavier silk. It was way too long. She tied a cord around my waist and bloused the excess fabric over it. Then she wrapped a stiff obi waistband around me and fastened it with two cords. The obi was wide and uncomfortable. I felt like I was dressed in a set of heavy theater curtains. The maid, however, seemed pleased. She escorted me to my grandmother, presented me shyly, and left. I took my place across the table. We sat on zabuton cushions placed on the tatami. The doors had been opened to let in a breeze. A lantern glowed palely just outside the entrance, shadowed by the dance of moths and other bugs attracted to the light. The pungent scent of kitori senco, mosquito coil placed to ward off the insects, perfumed the air. We sat at the low table, with chopsticks, eating white rice and nori, thin green-black squares of pressed seaweed, sere, and stiff-starched as parchment. We held the nori over a candle flame to toast. An occasional rag-winged moth, drawn by the flame of our candles, circled and expired. The corpses of moths were soon scattered over the table like dried petals. Beautiful bowls, painted with fish and flowers and filled with unidentifiable foodstuffs covered the table. Grandmother ate with great relish, but only one of the dishes was appealing to me; in a blue, stork-patterned bowl, everyday hothouse cucumbers floated in saltwater, peeled and sliced. Because I knew what they were, I ate these, with the white rice and the squares of crisped, tasteless nori. Grandmother noticed my selectivity with a diffident snort that I interpreted as affection. I wanted to think she approved.

That night, in between the Katan's cry and the bell-cricket's liin-liin-liin, I heard the long, ragged sound of Grandmother's coughing sawing through the velvet darkness. One, two, three, four, on and on, on and on like sheep plunging fearfully over the dream-haunted precipice.

For weeks I lived like a ghost speaking to almost no one. I went to the store, alone, to buy Grandmother's bread. I found a park nearby with a well and shrine where I could sit by myself for hours. I found a library full of Japanese books, none of which I could read. The texts were like hieroglyphics, a wall that I still couldn't climb over. I met a girl who lived in the apartment next door. Her name was Satchko, and she was nine. She had an older sister, Miki, who was fourteen years old. Miki wore straight skirts and shoes with short heels when she wasn't in school, and I wanted very much to impress her.

Miki treated Satchko and me with the tender disdain that one should reserve for babies. I was ashamed of my friendship with Miki's kid sister, so in the end, I avoided them both. But Satchko was very persistent, and I was so lonely that I would eventually seek out her company.

Some evenings Satchko and I would watch Japanese TV together. The sound of the shows would float out of the open window and up over Grandmother's garden wall to escape and join the noise of her neighborhood—the twangy voices of Japanese singers on the variety shows or the sing-song of the sumo referee's voice as he introduced the wrestlers. The sumo wrestlers were enormous, near-naked men whose goal was to push one another out of a ring. Most of what we saw were the bare backsides of their thunderous haunches bisected by a meaningless thong. Grandmother also loved this sport, but I don't think Sara would have allowed me to watch it.

I was especially fond of movies with dangerous ninja, assassins dressed all in black. Their faces were masked, and they carried razor-sharp shurukin, star-shaped daggers that they threw in great quantities at superhuman speed, jumping backward up into the fruitless black-branched trees, their laughter hollow, ringing in empty forests, while the hero spun around and around trying to find them, brows knitted, his long dark hair swinging across his face, catching his mouth, his sword gleaming, his pale hands clutching it fiercely, pulling it over his head in an arc.

Sometimes I would sit and stare at the Japanese characters and the bland, smiling faces in Grandmother's magazines which, curiously, one must read from back to front. Though it didn't matter; I didn't know what I read. I went with Grandmother to the bank or with the maid to the market.

I stood in the garden and watched them at work, their bonneted heads bent over flower beds. Haruka, Grandmother's maid, said:

"Heaven and earth are flowers—

God, as well as Buddha, are flowers.

The heart of man is also the soul of flowers."

I was surely disappointing my grandmother in just about every way. I knew nothing about bulbs or perennials; about bonsai, the pines and cedars that they purposefully dwarfed, or ikebana, flowers arranged—yin/yang, sun/moon—in a manner that supposedly mirrors the world.

———

Gene had left the city for a while on business. I stayed on, my grandmother's hostage, while Sara, having sacrificed me for her freedom from Grandmother, played house in a Japanese hotel and shepherded her children across town in a series of taxis and buses. Most of my days were passed in solitude. Grandmother could only handle children two-at-a-time, having only two hands to drag them about, and she wasn't fond of misbehaved children.

The days seemed to creep by. Then, suddenly, it was early August. All around us the city was celebrating: O-Bon, (the Festival of the Dead), Mamemaki (the bean-strewing), and the myriad tiny regional festivals—Shinto, Buddhist, and Zen—that are observed in all quarters in a metropolis as varied as Tokyo. We got used to the click of dragon's teeth, to the evil grimaces of little ivory devil heads with ruby-colored glass eyes. Phosphorescent paper obake, female ghosts with long dark hair, footless, their kimonos disappearing into smoky whiffs, dangled in all of the ten-yen shops. Because they glowed eerily in the dark, Samuel, Mimi, and Gray loved these and bought them by the score. They scared one another moaning "Obaaakeeee" in deep, spooky voices and told each other progressively more frightening stories.

We lived in the shadow of the Kabuki-za—the classical Japanese theater. Grandmother loved the stage. She'd once been an actress in the Takarazuka, an all-female theater. Ghost stories were a part of both traditions, and she and Sara loved to tell them.

In the spirit of O'Bon, Grandmother, forgetting her ban against English, told us *Yotsuya Kaidan,* a particularly grisly tale.

We were in Grandmother's parlor, sitting on some silk futons and zabutons that Sara's tailor had just delivered. It was humid that day. Everything smelled faintly of mildew. Unlike Sara, Grandmother had a thick Japanese accent, so even though she told it in English, the story had a strange, foreign sound.

"Iyemon was an evil man," she began, "a ronin, a maverick samurai, forced by the great economic grindstone to earn his living as a maker of oil paper umbrellas."

Grandmother spoke with savage certainty. A fierce gleam came into her eye. "The samurai were once a powerful class. When the reformation took away their masters, a dreadful force was unleashed. We are a samurai family," she said, looking directly at me. "Our code is one of honor and strength. This you mustn't forget."

She continued in a colder and quieter tone. "Iyemon had fallen so low that his only redeeming virtue was his lovely wife, Oiwa. So selfless and pure was Oiwa that she had given this bad man a child. Just as a lotus opens in mud, grace can descend and flower even among demons. But in this world, wickedness often rules. Unbeknownst to the delicate Oiwa, her husband had murdered her father, his father-in-law, because the old man was privy to his darker past.

"Were these crimes enough? Not at all. Tempted further by passion, Iyemon was seduced by the youth of his neighbor's granddaughter. She, foolish girl, was in love with him, too, and wanted nothing more than to marry him. So, at the urging of the girl's grandfather (Iyemon needed little convincing), Iyemon administered a 'blood-road-medicine' to his ailing wife. Oiwa thought this was a potion to strengthen her after the birth of her child. In reality, it was a poison. Its purpose was to put an end to her life!

"Poor Oiwa," Grandmother keened. "She had no idea why she grew weaker and weaker. She was so ashamed that she did not quickly recover to perform her service as wife. And her baby died, because when it drank the milk from her breast, it drank poison, too. Imagine the mother's sorrow. Her own milk, she thought, had sealed her child's doom. She sank into deepest despair.

"An old masseur took pity on Oiwa. Taking her to a mirror, the good servant showed her the truth. But the truth is not always a pretty thing. Oiwa's beautiful face and figure had been deformed by the poison. The black waterfall of her hair had vanished. In its place was baldness and a few stringy wisps. She had lost her teeth to the terrible drugs. One eye was so swollen that it couldn't be opened. Iyemon had turned her into a monster!"

Grandmother paused dramatically, lips pursed. Mimi whimpered and grabbed for my hand, her fingers locking on mine. The rest of us sat in horrified silence. Reassured that the performance was having the proper results, Grandmother went on.

"How often we find that sentiments reflect the vessel that holds them. Iyemon had tainted Oiwa with his evil. Her emotions took on the hideous shape of her disfigurement. She was filled with hatred and the desire for revenge. But, a spirit as sweet as Oiwa's could not inhabit the same frame as these ugly emotions. So the gentle Oiwa died at last. However, her brutal resentment remained.

"Iyemon's crime did not go unwitnessed. His servant, Kobo-tokei Kohei, knew of his wicked act. But, a guilty man buries the truth, so Iyemon murdered him, too, on the trumped-up excuse of theft. The servants of terrible masters are doomed.

"Iyemon nailed the body of Oiwa to one side of a board, Kohei to the other, and set it adrift on a river. He was free, at last, to satisfy his desires and marry the young girl next door.

"How very surprised Iyemon was," Grandmother said in her best Kabuki-style sing-song, "when he raised the veil of his beautiful bride and saw, instead of the girl, the disfigured face of Oiwa. With a samurai's lightning speed, he drew his sword and severed the head.

"How shocked he was, when the ghost of his servant, Kohei, blocked his flight. He thought not a minute, but cut that head off as well.

"And then, oh, it was the worst surprise of all! For Iyemon had not killed the ghosts of Oiwa and Kohei. No, in reality, he had slain his neighbor and his new child-bride!

"Where can a man like Iyemon escape from these terrible deeds? Oiwa's tortured face, the proof of his vile work, appeared to him everywhere—in the river where he had thrown the bodies, in the lantern trailing hairlike tresses of smoke that swayed over his head. He could not even hide on Hebiyama, Snake Mountain, far from all men. All of nature abhorred him and rose up to accuse him.

"Isn't it, finally, an act of kindness that his brother-in-law found him and killed him, thus ending the cycle of terror? Perhaps not. Perhaps Iyemon's horror continues with this story. But, the spirits of the dead are avenged when we tell it, and the natural order restored."

Inspired by Grandmother's narrative, Sara told us the story of Takatasama and the Terrible Mask. Mr. Takata was Grandmother's second husband.

"Hanabe Furigawa, your grandmother," Sara began in her best bedtime-story voice, "was, in her youth, a great beauty. Having run away, at an early age, from the imprisoning responsibilities of a powerful family, she became an actress, forsaking the world of duty for one of pleasure. Men loved her and she loved them, finding in the sensual world her supreme satisfaction. But, being of an old and honorable family, she could never forsake her disciplines. These came to center around her appearance. Milk baths, oatmeal scrubs, salt rubs, and rose water were all part of her arsenal. Her beauty was maintained through a regime so exacting that it went from the realm of art to that of religion."

Sara looked over at Grandmother and cleverly arched an eyebrow. Grandmother gave the slightest of nods bidding Sara to continue her tale.

"Hanabe-san was really so lovely that she got all the leads in the plays. Conquering hearts in the same way, she also got all the leading men and had plenty of ardent fans. Thus, she had her pick of fine husbands, selecting and marrying three men in the course of her flamboyant career. All three were men of style and great wealth—one Japanese and two European—but no man was more dazzled by Hanabe-san's beauty than Mr. Takata, her second husband. He knew nothing of her maintenance program, being generally away on endless business that added to his already monumental wealth and to the stress that he was continually under. His health, as a result, was not good. His only relaxation was in returning to the arms of his elegant wife, to the effortless radiance that was his greatest inspiration.

"Coming home one night, a few days early from a business trip, Takata-san breathed his usual sigh of relief. Thinking it late and not wanting to disturb Hanabe-san's slumbers, he crept through the house. He entered the darkened bedroom with his hat still on and his briefcase still in his hands. Hanabe-san was not sleeping at all. She was in the middle of her secret beauty routine. Thinking she'd heard a burglar, she bolted out of her bed. That is where she was when Mr. Takata saw her, a tall figure in her ghost-white pajamas. Her face was completely covered in a mixture of pressed tomatoes and clotted cream. The cucumber slices that covered her eyes had started a ghoulish slide down her cheeks. She recognized her husband and screamed, probably more so than she would have had he been a burglar. Expecting his lovely wife and faced, instead, with this frightening apparition, Takata-san also let out a scream. It was said that this shock nailed the lid on his coffin. The "unmasking" as Hanabe-san came to call it, seemed to weaken Takata-san's constitution. He was never the same again. Nor, for that matter, was the marriage, for your Grandmother never forgave him."

Grandmother's maid, Haruka, appeared with refreshments. I could tell that she had been listening, too, maybe hiding behind the sliding door to the parlor. Grandmother and Sara sipped dark green tea, studying the way the leaves fell and rose and fell again, swirling once, twice, on their perfect journey through the cup. Mimi, Samuel, Gray, and I drank milky brown tea sweetened with plenty of sugar. Refreshed by the tea and inspired by the contemplative spirit that had settled upon our circle, Sara told us the story of Senjin-san's Ghost.

Senjin-san was our youngest uncle. He lived, as he always had, in northern Japan on the family lands in Akishima.

Known for his gambling, carousing, and fondness for women, he always seemed to find the best parties, even in that pastoral part of the world. Coming home late one rainy night from just such an affair, with a burp on his lips and a belly full of rice wine, he stopped at the side of the deserted country road to relieve himself and was filling a ditch with a powerful sake-laced stream when a beautiful woman came out of nowhere. She begged him to help her, claiming that someone was trying to kill her. In an uncharacteristically ungentlemanly fashion, perhaps brought on by his boisterous nature, perhaps by the wine, Senjin-san ignored her plea and lunged at her instead. He fought hard to win her, but she was unyielding. The next morning, two neighborhood boys found him on that muddy path complaining loudly, wet and disruptive, with his head firmly stuck in the fork of a tree.

He said he'd been tricked by a kami, or spirit. No one believed him. But, Senjin-san stuck to his story, even going so far as to dig up from the local shimbun-sha, the newspaper office, a surprising old story about a young woman of fine birth who'd been dragged to the very spot and murdered by robbers. He was convinced that the ghost of this lady, in quest for revenge against the abuses of men, had appeared to him and misled him, turning herself into a tree, compromising him and cluttering this transformation and his entrapment with innuendo. He insisted that his humiliating discovery was her form of punishment. Other times, he changed his story completely and claimed that kitsune, the shape-shifting fox, had changed itself into a woman and teamed up with a badger, another magical animal, to trick him. He was fondest of telling this tale when he had been drinking awhile.

Mimi, Samuel, and Gray were still living in the children's dormitory of the Daimyô Hotel. The constant presence of goblins, demons, and gods seemed to have had an affect on them. I wondered if the demons weren't winning. Transformed by these stories and by our surroundings, drunk with mystery and with their fear, Samuel, Mimi, and Gray hid behind curtains when they could find them, jumped out from behind tables and screens, did Frankenstein imitations, and ran yelling through the treasured vegetable garden of one of Grandmother's unfortunate neighbors. The woman would run from her house brandishing her gardening shears, crying helplessly, "Warui, warui, wampaku-na, kodomo-tachi-me! Wicked, wicked, naughty devil-children!" She would take her stand, a ferocious guardian, next to her trampled eggplant. The ground around her feet was littered with the delicate purple blossoms.

"Yes, you had better run, you evil things, because when I catch you, I will cut off your ears and make them into pickle pots."

We danced around in the streets whenever anyone else in the city did, buying festival foods or candies with clear rice-paper wrappers that had to be sucked off, standing in huge crowds, stretching high on our toes, hoping for dragons, drums, or priests in white or priests in bright orange or half-clad young men with sticks and dances; singing, chanting with a breathless crowd, yearning for golden shrines, colored paper, the ritual scattering of rice or salt or blood-red beans.

I was also reeling under the influence of the confusing, multilayered world around me. I struggled without direction through a landscape mined with disturbing surprises and few explanations against a backdrop of Ukiyoye, floating world pictures—woodcuts of geisha and kabuki actors plying their trade—the very real vision of pale women dressed only in steam in the great Tokyo bathhouses that I visited with Sara and Grandmother or of the park-like shrines tended by silent, white-shrouded priests.

One afternoon, I followed a procession on its sinuous journey through the labyrinth of Tokyo streets. The Shinto priests were moving a shrine through their parishes. The shrine was the chosen home of a kami, or spirit. The kami was represented only by this golden abode and its talisman, a wooden paddle upon which was written a mysterious Japanese character. The shrine was balanced on a glittering palanquin that rested on the specially chosen shoulders of six of the district's most handsome young men. They were dressed only in loincloths. White headbands circled their foreheads. Their dark hair rose over their headbands like spiky cockscombs.

In this way, the shrine spirit visited all of its worshippers, spreading blessings. And, in this way, the celebrants honored the kami.

"Wasshoi! Wasshoi! Wasshoi!" chanted the young men as they ran through the neighborhoods with the precious palanquin on their shoulders. They had a lot of ground to cover.

"Wasshoi! Wasshoi! Wasshoi!" the wild throng screamed back.

"Wasshoi! Wasshoi! Wasshoi!" I heard myself yelling as I tried to hang onto the dragon's tail, the end of a parade that zig-zagged through every lane and alleyway in the district.

I wanted to look into the shrine. I wanted to see the kami.

"What does this kami look like?" I wondered. Was it male or female? Beautiful or scary? I tried to get closer, but it was unapproachable. It bobbed on before me on the shoulders of the six young men threading their way through an ecstatic crowd.

Hands waved in the air. People jostled and pushed. It was too confusing. The dragon was moving too quickly. I lost hold of its tail. I got tangled up in the mob that milled about in the streets. The voices of the young men moved further and further away, and I found myself in an unfamiliar part of the city, much dingier than the places to which I was accustomed.

Suddenly, I was alone. I trotted along a sidewalk bordered by a ditch in which raw sewage flowed. Cheap nawa-noren, rope blinds, covered the entrances of the dirty soba-ya stalls, taishu-shoku-do, and sushi stalls. I passed derelict ten-yen stores and closed restaurants with chipped maneki-neko, good luck cats, beckoning in their grimy windows. The air smelled like sour milk and garbage. A baby wailed. It might have been a cat. It was a long, twisting cry. I wondered where it had come from.

A very muscular Japanese woman in a thigh-high pink dress leaned in one of the doorways. Her long, yellow-shinned legs were bare. To her left was a mountain of empty beer bottles, brown and long-necked, their labels a flashy Sapporo-red. She nudged the pile with the toe of her pink, high-heeled shoe as I passed. The bottles tumbled and clattered, rolling in all directions. Swaying on her high heels, the woman moved in on my flank.

"Michi-ni-mayottano? Are you lost?" she asked in a curious way.

She had a young, well-formed face, but her skin wasn't good and she wore too much makeup.

I nodded.

Then her red lips pulled back in a leer and she lifted her skirt. She had nothing on underneath, and I saw that she wasn't a woman at all, but a man. She puckered her lips up in a monkey-like grimace that was meant to parody a kiss. Then she laughed. I turned and fled. I heard her laughter ringing behind me in the empty streets as I ran.

I tried to retrace my steps, circling back and back. Finally finding a landmark, a familiar shop, I slowly reconstructed the path that I'd followed, but it did not seem that I was heading home at all. The vision of the woman pulling the short pink dress up over a penis swam before me. I followed that image as it receded in the dusk toward a darkened lintel, the portal of Grandmother's house.

4

himawari |
sunflowers

Gene returned in late August, and we moved north to a pink house he'd bought in the country on the perimeter of an enormous sunflower field. Gene had a job with a company that was building bridges for an American outpost at the northern tip of Honshu—a place full of soldiers, airstrips, weapons, and dazed farmers. To the west across the Sea of Japan, Russia, China, and North Korea kissed on a desolate border just south of Vladivostok.

"Another frontier," Sara said tiredly, surveying our new surroundings.

"It's beautiful country," Gene laughed. "Sara, you shine in rough territory."

"Right," Sara said irritably. "Annie Oakley. Calamity Jane."

"You used to love it, Sara," Gene teased.

I vaguely remembered. It was true. We'd settled, in the past, on some pretty rugged terrain—what Sara called "god-forsaken country." We lived in Indonesia when I was Mimi's age, while Gene built bridges all over the Pacific. My earliest memories were of a bungalow on the edge of an orangutan forest. There was a wire fence around our compound to keep us in and the orangutans out. Orangutans used to come right up to the fence. They were shaggy and orange and had big, simple faces. Even the little ones were huge. Sara worried constantly that they'd carry off one of her babies. She used to throw empty baby food jars at them to chase them away. But they loved the smell of the baby food, so they kept coming back.

"I never liked it," Sara insisted.

"Liar," Gene chuckled. "You loved it."

"No," Sara argued. "You loved it."

"I love you, Sara," Gene said. "I love you in spite of the kids, the marriage, your mother. I love you in spite of my infidelities, in spite of the way people live and die and lie."

"I know. I know," Sara mumbled. "But, Gene, can you love me in spite of the money?" Sara's eyes looked troubled. She looked like Mimi. At that moment I saw how much like Mimi she was. "Will you be able to see past the money to the woman on the other side?"

"I don't know, Sara," he said sadly, hanging his head. "We'll have to see. I can try." Then he smiled and broke into a chorus of "Buffalo Gal," his voice low and inviting. Sara relaxed a little. His arm went around her waist. He pulled her close so that their chests touched, pressing her against him.

"Buffalo Gal, wont'cha come out tonight?" he crooned swaying from side to side, guiding Sara's body with his. "Come

out tonight, come out tonight." They danced in the garden—
Gene singing softly and leading, Sara following. Samuel and
Gray, pleased with this physical turn of events, added their
voices to Gene's. "Buffalo gal, wont'cha come out tonight?"
they serenaded.

I felt Mimi thrust her tiny brown hand into mine.

"And dance by the light of the moon," she piped in, tugging
irresistibly at me. I, too, gave in to the music, to the soft
chant of Gene's voice and Sara's hypnotic compliance. I
joined the other five dancers, two-stepping behind Mimi,
Samuel, and Gray, promenading along the fence.

"Oh, wont'cha, wont'cha, wont'cha, wont'cha come out
tonight," we all sang, dancing—a strange troupe capering
about in the raggedy garden in that "god-forsaken country."
And the light grew weaker around us as we danced, and our
voices rose up into the dusk.

The pink house had a garden all around it with flowers and a
white picket fence and a carport in which to park our station
wagon, Gene's newly acquired antique Edsel, the snarl of bicycles, and Mimi's trike. There were four or five sheds for stor-
age—also painted pink. These sheds were like little houses. One
was used as a clubhouse by Samuel and Gray; the others were
filled with old newspapers, magazines, and spiders.

The little pink house seemed smaller still because it was
filled with four children, two parents, a grandmother, a maid,
and a rabbit. Samuel and Gray shared a room, Mimi and I
shared a room, Sara and Gene shared a room, Grandmother
had her own room, the rabbit stayed outside, and the maid

cycled in to work on the rutted country roads every day. When it was raining or snowing, Gene would pick her up in the station wagon or take her home with her rickety bicycle thrown in the back. I loved to watch her come cycling toward the house in the morning. She wore a triangular scarf tied over her short black hair. Made from the same fabric as her apron, it was white and studded with pale blue cornflowers.

Her name was Ineko-san, and she called all of us by our regular names with "chan " on the end, which is the way they address children in Japan. She had two gold teeth in the front of her mouth and a broad face with very red cheeks. Sara said that Ineko-san was extremely healthy from riding her bicycle all the time. When Ineko-san was embarrassed, which happened often, the red on her cheeks would bloom until her whole face, otherwise white as milk, was a rosy pink. I thought this was amazing and beautiful. Her hands were large and also red. She had a gold wedding ring on the left one.

Ineko-san was busy all day, cleaning and picking up after us and keeping an eye on the rabbit, which was her gift to Mimi. She didn't know how to cook. If we asked her for something to eat, her solution was always the same—peanut butter and jelly sandwiches. We soon quit asking. Mimi, however, loved peanut butter and jelly sandwiches, a passion that Ineko-san shared. The sweet, sugary sandwiches were a delicacy in Japan where peanut butter was an exotic substance. In the middle of the day, they would sit together, eating sandwiches at the kitchen table, as if it were an island, and they were the only two people in the world.

The house, which Gene had bought from an American, was western-style, except for a few sliding doors and the traditional genkan. The Japanese builders had insisted on those. The bathroom was a cavernous stone room with an old ringer washer on one end and a concrete and tile bathtub big enough to swim laps in on the other. Because of its size, it was impossible to fill. The hot water was exhausted before it was three inches deep. So Sara had a wall constructed across the tub, and we filled only one part with water. The other part was never used. Like Grandmother, Sara believed in very hot baths. The bathroom would fill up with steam when we used it, and the tiled floor would quickly grow slippery. Sara threw towels all over the floor while her children jumped in and out of the tub, wriggling and squirming, pink as peeled shrimp.

Gray spent a lot of his time in the bathroom. He was fascinated with the old ringer washer. It was one of the few machines in our old-fashioned house. He would hang around whenever Ineko-san did laundry, watching her feed the wet clothes that churned around in the washer into the ringer. It pressed them flat as boards and dropped them, stiff and dry, into the basket below. He stayed out of trouble for hours, entranced by the brown water that gushed from the rubber hose into a drain on the bathroom floor. He even managed to persuade Ineko-san to let him climb on a stool once or twice, pull the wet clothes out, and feed them into the ringer—a process for which he still had to stand tiptoe. Sara warned Ineko-san to watch him closely. She was afraid he might lose his balance and tumble head-first into the murky washwater and drown.

As usual, Sara's worries proved well-founded. We were horrified one day, when Ineko-san had the washer running, to hear Gray's piercing screams emerge from the bathroom along with the deep "rum-rum" of the machine. Ineko-san, who had left him alone there, grew pale as paper, and we all ran—mother, maid, and children—to the quarry-like room. Ineko-san was the first to enter. She shrieked. Then we pushed through the doorway only to see Gray, his eyes huge, his face a mask of terror, his toes barely touching his stool, watching his arm disappear through the ringer. Tears ran down his face, probably more from the shock than the pain, and the fear of what the dreadful ringer would do when it came, at last, to his head. Sara and Ineko-san dashed across the room with a cry, Ineko-san nearly taking a fall on the slippery tile floor. Simultaneously, they hurled themselves at the lever to turn off the machine. They were successful. It groaned to a halt, and for a few minutes the only sounds in the room were Gray's choking sobs, as Sara and Ineko-san pried wide the rubber rollers and pulled back his arm.

Sara scolded him between hugs, and Ineko-san prattled unhappily in Japanese, "Oku-san, gomen-nasai. Kawaisoni, Gray-chan. Kawaisoni-ne." Oh, Madame, I'm so sorry. Poor little Gray. Poor, poor little Gray.

Samuel, Mimi, and I, standing helplessly at the door, watched the big round tears roll down Gray's cheeks, his arm an angry red, the women fussing over him, the diabolical

machine behind him, and we began to laugh. We laughed sur-
reptitiously at first, the way we did in church, and then, hys-
terically, as we deserted the doorway, afraid of Sara's wrath.
We could not look at Gray for days without laughing.

Grandmother did not like the house. I'm sure she regretted
acquiescing to Sara's pleas to move north with us. Even ill, she
must have felt she was far better off on her own in Tokyo. She
had packed her bags grudgingly, placing her brushes and combs
and nightclothes carefully into her crocodile valise. Her expression had been dour when Haruka, her maid, tearful and fussy
about being left behind, fluttered around the room, punctuat-
ing the movements of packing with laments, little sighs, and the
ubiquitous shaking of her head to and fro, like a large flower
on a too-slender stem. Grandmother gave her a peremptory
"thank you," an envelope thick with money. Haruka sniffed and
the two women parted, never to see one another again.

Grandmother said little on the train, sitting up in the night
compartment where she must have caught a chill, while the
Japanese countryside flashed past, pinned for the moment
under the eery glow of the train's lights.

Did she shudder when she saw the dilapidated pink house
in that lonely corner of northern Japan? She merely pulled
her sweater more closely about her, against the cool northern evening, and crossing the threshold, asked stiffly to be
shown to her room.

After that, Grandmother rarely left her quarters, preferring
not to have to pick her way around children and their clutter.
Her room smelled of medicine, of tokohon, the white squares

of medicated plasters that she wore on her wrists and arms. The signs of her illness became more pronounced. She got up often from her bed to pace. Her legs, wrapped in a pale green robe, seemed to be faintly blue—all bones and tendons. Whenever I was forced to enter her room, she would stand in one corner, her lips pursed critically, and watch me closely, as though she were trying to form a question that she couldn't quite articulate.

By one of those gross miscalculations that mystified me, some of my clothing had been stowed in a dresser in Grandmother's bedroom. This was the same cherrywood dresser my things had occupied in her Tokyo house. The dresser was placed under a large window that framed a wild tract of uncultivated land. Grandmother did not much care for this view, so the curtains were usually drawn. I had to go often into Grandmother's room to gather my things. Once there, I was obligated to pay my respects. I would sit in the armchair beside her bed and rattle on idly in English until she clipped short the senseless run of my conversation.

"Ki-ga tarun deru kara yo," she'd say.

I considered this to be the equivalent to being excused.

Once, I asked Sara what it meant.

Sara looked baffled. "Are you sure that's what she said?"

"Yes. Ki-ga tarun deru kara yo," I repeated.

Sara frowned. "How very strange," she said. "Your grand-mother told you your soul is small."

Unlike Grandmother, Samuel, Mimi, and Gray were ecsta-tic about our new home. There was not much time left

before we had to start school and all around us the countryside stretched like an open hand. Acres of furrowed, black
earth encircled us and from it emerged a seven-foot sea of
sunflowers that hemmed our house in. The country roads
and paths looked like grooves cut into a maze. On the other
side of the field was the tiny bud of a forest where the
farmer's ramshackle compound sprawled, the primitive
equipment rusting and scattered about. Beyond that, beyond
our squint through the clear farm light gathering over the
distance like a curtain of haze, was a tiny machi, a little
Japanese town littered with buildings of secondhand wood
and thatch. It was peopled with children with red-chapped
cheeks, and rubber-booted women like Ineko-san, their hair
tucked under bright cotton scarves. Wary-footed kittens
capered on little legs, unsure, we thought, of whether they
would serve as a pet or somebody's soup stock. There was
the fragrance of noodles frying; of rich fishy broths that perfumed the air. There was always plenty of laughter and good-
natured teasing when the scruffy American children rolled
into town on their bikes. Past the criss-cross of dirt paths that
bordered this town, tall, junk-cluttered weeds dotted more
farmfields, and these stretched on again, endlessly, so that we
wondered, without hope, if one ever finally got to the end of
the world.

Into this landscape Mimi was always threatening to run
away. Something had happened to her in Tokyo. Perhaps one
of the oni had captured her spirit and still held her a prisoner
in its ugly embrace. She had earned the nickname "Fugu," or

Blowfish, from Grandmother, for her petulance. She could be poisonous. She was a tough little five-year-old, used to rejection. She tagged doggedly behind Samuel and Gray, only to be refused admittance to their clubhouses and access to their baseball gloves, bats, and bikes. Sometimes, they would condescend to her, and she would be allowed to follow along with them, running whatever menial errands they might contrive, grave with her great responsibility. This devotion to the boys was fostered by the circumstances of our environment. She had no other playmates. There were so few children around of her age, and none that she held in the same respect that she had for Samuel and Gray.

"No, you can't come."

Samuel and Gray looked down imperiously at her from their bicycle seats, their feet planted on the dusty pedals.

"You're too slow."

Mimi had dragged her bike with the training wheels around to the front of the house. It sputtered and rattled on the gravel drive. Samuel was leaning body and bike against the Easter-egg blue hood of Gene's Edsel, looking through the half-closed lids of his hazel eyes at the cards she'd attached to the spokes of her rear wheels with clothespins to make a motor sound.

"Go take care of your rabbit," he breathed, and she knew at once that this was an order and that he would not relent.

"Hurry up, Sam," Gray urged, guiding his bike carefully through the narrow passage between the white picket fence and the car.

"I'm coming," Samuel said savagely, his body already swinging away from the car, onto the bike, turning, pushing into the pedals, the gravel driveway exploding under his wheels.

It had not been a good week for Mimi. Samuel and Gray had found three new American boys. This meant an entire ritual of familiarization. They would have to take the new boys out to show them the lay of the land, how far their territories stretched, where the boundaries were, and maybe, if they liked the new boys, where to find badgers and how to cajole the farmer into giving them rides on his plow horse.

Mimi kicked off her slip-on Batman shoes at the genkan, sending one flying against the front door. She dragged her pink-stockinged feet slothfully across the carpet to the kitchen, and leaning on everything, winding her thin brown arms around the chairs, asked Ineko-san for some food for her rabbit. Ineko-san was just sweeping some of the shredded, wet newspaper she used instead of a mop out the door.

"Mimi-chan, peanut-buttah-jelly?" she asked energetically in response to Mimi's request for food.

"No, Ineko-san," Mimi said roughly, "For my rabbit. You know, usagi."

"Ah, rah-beet," Ineko-san nodded, scooping some rolled oats out of a jar, bagging them and pulling the discolored leaves of a faded head of lettuce out of the vegetable bin. We also fed the rabbit the thick, dreadful part of big carrots that's close to the top and very tough.

Mimi thrust the bag of oats under one arm, the old lettuce leaves under the other, and sticking her feet halfway into her shoes, clambered into the yard.

The rabbit's hutch sat in one corner of the garden, in the shade of one of the pink sheds, where the rabbit huddled, distrustfully chewing air. There were always big holes to be filled, dug under the rickety white fence adjacent to it, either by dogs or hungry rodents. We were never sure which. The rabbit stopped chewing as Mimi approached, its mad red eyes watching her closely, its long ears sheathed on either side of its head. Its nose wrinkled nervously. Then, again, it began its obsessive chewing. Mimi opened wide the mesh door of the hutch and reaching into the dank interior, drew the white, loose-boned body out with both arms.

"Come on, boy," she urged huskily.

The rabbit hung in her arms. It was nearly as big as she was, and its sudden movement could have sent her reeling.

"Good bunny," she whispered encouragingly.

Ineko-san's clean white sheets hung on the clothesline, dividing the yard into rooms. The rabbit hopped effortlessly from this place to that, in and out between the sheets, its nose moving feverishly to keep track of the girl's whereabouts.

Doors slammed. A loud commotion burst from the front of the house. Mimi jumped. The rabbit jumped. Samuel and Gray were back.

"Wow, I can't believe it! Can you believe it?" Samuel had flung his bike in the driveway and was tearing through the house.

"No, I can't believe it," Gray echoed, running his hand dramatically through his dark hair. "Wow, it's really incredible!"

Mimi tore off in the direction of the excitement, then remembering, ran back to where her rabbit munched shortsightedly, scooped him up, and thrust him into the hutch.

"God," she heaved, surprised for the first time by his size, and headed indoors.

Samuel and Gray had already stormed through the house and were in the process of ransacking the kitchen, opening cupboards and drawers, slamming them closed. They opened and shut the refrigerator. Ineko-san gave an anguished glance at her once-clean floors, but was too astonished to say anything. The boys had not bothered to take off their shoes, a bravado only possible because Sara happened to not be home. I was reading one of Gene's novels, a book by Frank Yerby, full of gore, but my brothers' activity was far more intriguing. Gray was juggling the items that Samuel had shoved upon him during their march. One hand grasped the edge of a flat cardboard box, the kind that soda cans come in. Samuel warned him not to crush it by carrying it under his arm. Wadded under the other arm was a faded yellow blanket. Mimi winced at the sight. It was hers. But she knew better than to say anything. Mimi had a strange way of developing relationships with inanimate objects, blankets in particular. Her first blanket had been a beautiful, satin-edged, blue one. She refused to be separated from it, and it deteriorated into a filthy gray rag. Eventually, Sara pried it from her under the pretext of washing it. Mimi's tearful eyes had grown wide when Sara took her to the dryer, and opening up the lint trap, drew out a long sheet of fluff.

"Oh no, Mimi, your blanket!" Sara exclaimed.

To Mimi's credit, she did not linger miserably over the lint. This time, she was even more mature.

"Hey, what's going on?" she chirped excitedly, relinquishing in that exclamation, all claim to the yellow blanket.

"Huh?" Samuel turned to her absently. He had not noticed her until then. He did not respond to her question. He ignored her. "Ineko-san, don't we have any food?" he demanded roughly, letting the door of the cupboard slam shut.

Mimi sidled up to Gray, who was feeling very important as the supply carrier.

"Did you guys find something?" she asked hoarsely, her dark eyes bright with excitement.

"Yeah." Gray's voice was hushed with an almost religious awe. Mimi was close to getting an answer.

"Gray," Samuel called, "I think this is all we have." In Samuel's hand was a package of hot dogs.

"Come on. Let's go."

Gray did not even pause. Samuel was nearly out the door, Gray behind him. Mimi ran after them.

"Hey, you guys," she shouted desperately from the door, trying hard not to sound weak, not to sound five. "What's going on?"

Samuel had picked up his bike and was pushing it up the drive. He looked back over his shoulder, and a ravishing smile spread across his face.

"Not far from the house," he yelled hurriedly. "The ditch by the blackberry hedge. Come on." Then he was gone.

Mimi, ecstatic, grabbed her bicycle and started pedaling, her thin scabby legs pumping furiously as she rattled along in their wake.

The puppy had been wrapped in a plastic bag, its four legs tied together, its muzzle bound with a piece of wire, and thrown into a ditch, but it had somehow managed to thrust its pointed nose through the plastic—maybe the sharpness of the wire had torn it—and it had lived and Samuel and Gray had found it.

It must have been part Spitz, a fluffy white dog that is common in Japan, a white snowball with that northern dog circle of a tail, except that it had the markings of a brown mask around its eyes. The boys let it lie for a while in the ditch, wrapped in the old yellow blanket, crooning to it and stroking it gently. Then they brought it back to the house in the box, hid it in one of the pink sheds, and tried to feed it the hot dogs. They named the puppy Soft. They wanted to keep it.

Samuel asked me what they should do. I was supposed to be the expert on Sara.

"Well," I said sagely, "Sara will probably say yes, but you have to wait for the right time."

The right time did not present itself that evening. The new American boys came to see the dog and hovered about the shed. It was like a nativity, as if the puppy had just been born. Samuel crept into the shed that night, defying the spiders, and sat up with it so that it wouldn't whine or howl. The next morning, Samuel, Mimi, and Gray woke up, as usual, long before Ineko-san had arrived and long before Sara was up. They had a conference, their heads touching, like football players in a huddle.

"Ellen, we're going to make Sara breakfast," Samuel confided.

"Good idea," I remarked.

They cooked scrambled eggs and toast, loaded it on a tray, picked a flower from the garden and asked for my opinion. They'd done an excellent job. The eggs were a little runny, but there was a linen napkin under the plate and another, folded, on the wrong side. They'd scooped jam onto the bread plate, included a pat of butter and added crystal-cut salt and pepper shakers. Mimi had contributed a dollop of peanut butter. I was amazed. I had not thought them capable of any finesse. Mimi stood at the door, holding the tray. Gray knocked softly.

"Come in." Sara's voice came from the other side of the door. She sounded rested. She was probably surprised that her children had stayed quiet for so long. She liked to sleep late and was rarely able to do it.

She must have gasped when Gray opened the door and Mimi appeared with the breakfast tray. The sunlight streamed in through the window. Her two youngest children stood before her like angels.

"Oh, you darling children," Sara said. "Come here."

She plumped up the pillows behind her and helped situate the tray on her lap. They'd dressed the tray with a tiger lily plucked from the garden.

"How beautiful," Sara exclaimed.

"We love you, Sara," Mimi and Gray said sweetly, each kissing her on a cheek.

"Well, let me eat this at once," she said cheerily, "so that it doesn't get cold."

Mimi and Gray wisely withdrew.

"She's eating!" they announced as they ran out of the room.

Meanwhile, Samuel had washed and dried the dog. Ineko-san, who always sided with the children in matters of the heart, arrived in time to help him finish the job and handle the cleanup.

The puppy sat on wobbly haunches in the middle of the kitchen. It looked like a cotton ball. Its golden eyes looked up at us from behind the brown mask. Its mouth was pulled back over its pink gums in a kind of smile.

Samuel went over it one more time with a towel, making sure it was totally dry. The puppy had to be perfect. Nothing must go wrong.

The puppy was quiet, squirming nose-first into the crook of Samuel's arm, so that only the curl of its tail protruded, a white fan turned into a hoop, looking strangely separate and pointless against the moment. Mimi and Gray disappeared into Sara's room and reappeared with the empty tray. Carrying the puppy, Samuel stepped into the room.

He did not pause.

"Look, Mother," he whispered, dumping the dog, in a bundle, onto Sara's lap. "We found him in a ditch, wrapped in a plastic bag, with wire wrapped around his nose and his feet tied. He almost died, Sara. We saved him." The dog struggled to its feet on the soft, rumply bedclothes. It climbed up Sara's chest and thrust its face into hers, looking ridiculous with its brown mask and that funny dog-smile that it had. Samuel sat beside Sara's bed, one arm draped over her, his hazel eyes and brown hair catching the sunlight that was racing into the room. He reached out, rubbed the dog's back, then he said simply, flatly, stating the obvious, the real reason for everything: "See, he's soft."

Samuel would never try to argue points with Sara. He would present her with indisputable facts instead. That is how he got through to her.

Sara looked at the puppy's face closely, as though she were searching for something. She stroked its smooth head and fuzzy body thoughtfully, testing the truth of Samuel's words.

"Yes," she said gently, lifting the little thing up before her, examining it very closely. "Yes, he is very soft."

Her eyes were perfect mirrors of Samuel's, these two who always understood one another completely.

"Well, what's his name?" she asked simply.

Samuel reached out, petting the dog, knowing it was to be his.

"Soft," he said. "We're calling him Soft."

5

Anne |

The name of my best friend was Anne. I met her at Mercy-Mary Catholic, the English girls' school to which we both commuted daily by train. I had distinguished myself in the first few weeks of school at Mercy-Mary Catholic at the Talent Parade, an all-student revue designed to showcase the new students' strengths. I did a big-lips imitation of Mick Jagger in concert. This was performed, of course, in school uniform since we weren't allowed anything as extravagant as costumes; but I was undeterred by my black shoes, white socks, and pleated, navy blue tunic, swiveling my hips and wrapping my mouth around the microphone so that it looked like I'd surely swallow it . . .

"I can't get no . . . satisfaction," I snarled, my long hair swinging as I swayed this way and that. The European nuns didn't like it. The Japanese nuns giggled. To my surprise they closed the curtain on me, but my gyrations and facial contortions did earn me a certain fame. I acquired an immediate following.

Anne had silky dark hair and wore short skirts and knee socks, later replaced by black stockings for which she was still very young, but they were woolen so she could convince her mother they were practical. Anne's mother was a doctor and her father an engineer. They were Japanese, but had lived a long time in Hawaii, so Anne's English was flawless, though laced with Americanisms. Her mother's English was very British, but her father's was fast and sassy. That was the kind of English Anne liked to speak. Anne's mother felt that English schools would be best for Anne and that I would be a good influence on her daughter. Sara agreed with Mrs. Matsuda, never questioning whether Anne might have the opposite influence on me.

Anne was attracted to me because of my stage performance. I was attracted to Anne on account of her colorful hairbands and the red velvet bows that she wore in her hair. They stood out against the sea of black hairbands, white blouses, and the navy blue plaid of our box-pleated tunics. When Mrs. Matsuda was away on business, Anne would show up at school in bright-colored shifts that matched her hairbands. She'd end up in the Superior's office, but she'd do it again the next time her mother was out of town. Anne said I looked drab in the conservative uniforms that I wore with unvarying sameness. Sara let me help select the fabrics from big bolts in the dressmaker's shop, but the styling was always the same. She was a product of harsh boarding schools. She believed in tunics and boxpleats for schoolgirls.

Anne and I hated the girls' school. We despised the oppressive nuns. They were big ugly women mainly from German, Dutch, and English families. A few of the Sisters were Japanese, but they didn't seem to enjoy the same status as the European nuns. They were lightweights—too pretty to ever be taken seriously. We didn't want to attend the Catholic school. We wanted to go to the school near the American airbase. It seemed so breezy and loose. It was closer to home. It was free. But Sara was adamant about the disciplines of a Catholic school, and how much better it was for me. So, I told Sara that the Sisters looked at me strangely, that it made me uncomfortable. I knew from the stories she'd told that Sara had something like that in her past—a boarding school nightmare even more unpleasant than dormitories, blancmange, and hickory-stick canings. It wouldn't take much to trigger those memories. It worked. She and Gene decided that my next school year would be at the American School. My transfer was the talk of Mercy-Mary Catholic. Girls cornered me in the halls to ask me how I'd managed to get out of the prison.

"My mother believes in more freedom," I lied.

I told Anne the truth.

Her response was intense.

"You've engineered both our escapes," she said gravely. "My mother will copy Sara."

Anne was right. Mrs. Matsuda made the announcement a few weeks after my parents made theirs. It was settled. Both Anne and I would attend the American school in the fall.

There was, of course, the problem of the superior standards of the Catholic school. This was handled by pushing both of us forward a grade, so that rather than going to the sixth grade, we were enrolled in the seventh. At the American school, seventh grade was considered part of the high school. Naturally, we found this jump in status extremely exciting.

Anne and I were perfectly matched. We were both the children of preoccupied parents. Mr. and Mrs. Matsuda were preoccupied with their jobs. Anne was an only child. Sara and Gene were preoccupied with trying to understand one another. Anne and I thrived on this absence of supervision. No one had time to take us anywhere, so we learned to use the local army of Japanese cabs, squandering allowances that were lavish by Japanese standards. The drivers came to know us and eventually took us here and there without even charging, though their generosity may have masked ulterior motives.

Unsupervised, we infiltrated the noisy Pacheco Palace where young Japanese hoodlums guzzled beer and sake-sotted old men watched their yen and their lives disappear into the raucous digestive systems of row-upon-row of pinball machines. We could also see any movie we wanted. There were no restrictions at the Japanese theater, although most of the movies were extremely lewd and obviously not for young girls. I remember one in which a man pierced his nipples with needles and another in which a woman bit the testicles off a series of goats. The movies were foreign, subtitled in Japanese, which, in spite of my studies, I still could not read. They seemed to bear no connection with the world as we knew it. We wrinkled our noses and filed the images away, to be fished out later and reflected upon.

That summer, before we switched schools, I had my first professional hair cut. Anne was with me. Sara sent me to a Japanese beauty parlor, and I should have known by paging through the magazines as I waited that I wouldn't be pleased with the results. I should have known by the beauticians' bouffant hairdos. They cut and cut and curled and curled and wheeled me under an institution-green hair dryer shaped like a beehive. It was so hot that I thought it was going to melt the multitude of tiny pink and blue rollers with which they'd covered my head. I could smell my hair frying. I tried to distract myself from the burning smell by thumbing through more magazines. The same disquieting hairdos stared at me from the pages. Anne tried to talk to me but I couldn't hear her over the roar of the hair dryer.

I scrunched down in the chair to escape the searing heat, but the busty beautician kept coming back to me swinging her hips and checking under the dryer by pulling a lock of hair, which by now must have been bone dry, out from one of the curlers. Then she readjusted the dryer, pushing it down further over my head, until I couldn't sit up straight if I tried.

She finally finished teasing and torturing the hair of the woman she was working on and rolled me out from under the dryer and unwrapped my hair from the curlers. Then she took these coils and loops of hair and began to work furiously with a sticky blue spray that reminded me of starch and a rattail comb. She created a structure of hair not unlike the ones in the magazines. She laquered it with hairspray. In the end, I looked like someone had stuck a too-large wig on my head. Sara had given me money for the beautician's tip as well as the hair cut, but I decided to keep it, since she'd done such a bum job.

"Well, what do you think?" I asked Anne as we skipped through the shabby corridor of toy stores and noodle stalls that led from the beauty shop to the main street of the machi. I noticed that no matter how I moved my hair didn't.

"It makes you look older," Anne said.

Sara told me she loved my new hairstyle, but I suspected a lie. I think she thought it looked silly. I thought I caught her stifling a laugh.

Anne never committed to whether she liked it or not. It didn't matter. A few weeks later she had her hair done exactly like mine.

"Ellen, there's a giant fair in the machi," Anne announced definitively a week or two after that. Our hairdos, having collapsed under constant neglect, had resumed a more natural aspect. Anne was wearing a sundress and a pair of Mrs. Matsuda's biggest earrings. She was in a carnival mood. "Come on, let's go."

It was a soundless, white summer day, the kind that can easily deteriorate into tedium.

"All right," I agreed, twirling my pencil into my art-gum eraser. I was in the garden sketching the tiger lilies that had unfurled against the white picket fence. Black and gold garden spiders had thrown fragile webs up between the flowers. It was rare to see so many of the delicate spiders in the yard.

Mimi was fond of capturing them. She kept her spider-filled jars in the linen closet. Ineko-san let her do this because Mimi begged and the containers were all sealed. But a few weeks ago, the jars had been mysteriously separated from their lids. The spiders crawled out to hide or lay eggs in our clean sheets and pillowcases. Gray and Samuel ultimately confessed, but Mimi's jars of eight-legged pets were banned from the closet. Her pleading was useless. So, for a while at least, the spiders had a reprieve.

I liked the idea of the fair. There would be mask dancers, puppets, prizes, and games. There would be taiko drummers, ice milk, and sweet rice stands. The vendors would move their businesses outdoors. The streets would be lined with stalls selling trashy novelties.

"What's this fair about?" I asked.

"Oh, I don't know," Anne grimaced. "Flower Festival or something. It'll be fun. We can celebrate our graduation from MMC."

"Yeah," I said, "Mercy-Mother-Whack-it."

"Murder-Mother-Smack-it," Anne chanted along.

The festival must have been an important one. Streamers and kites filled the sky. Sloppy canopies of blue and pink paper flowers tented stands stacked with plastic dolls, watches, jewelry, and shoes. Uchiwa and sensu, round and folding fans, and parasols fluttered in doorways. Noisy knots of people clucked away happily with one another in Japanese. The songs of nasal radio crooners floated over the crowds.

We sampled yakitori—skewers of meats from a street vendor's cart. Sara had warned us against eating street food because it was unhealthy. That only made the soyu-drenched pork and chicken pieces doubly delicious. We stuffed ourselves on them.

"Oh, I feel just great. Don't you feel fantastic?" Anne sang into the air.

"Yes," I answered blithely. We were high on bad music and Meiji chocolate. At that moment in sunlight, under the china-blue sky, I loved Japan, too.

"I want to always remember this," Anne said, breathlessly. "We need something to remember this by."

She fixed her eyes on the corner of the trinket-loaded stand a few feet away. She was looking at a glittering pile of cheap, glass-studded brooches.

"We need rubies and sapphires," she said fiercely, and pushed me into the stand.

It was wobbly. I knocked over two trays of rings. The vendor started yapping and yelling at me. I saw Anne scoop up a few of the flashy pins. He saw her too. He tried to lunge past me, but thinking quickly, I blocked his way. He grabbed one of my wrists, his long fingernails digging into my flesh. Anne disappeared into the fair. Then, he turned to me, his skinny face full of malice.

"Dame-dame. Better not," I warned fearlessly, in my worst Japanese, surprising myself with my bravado.

He looked down at his brown claw, wrapped around my white wrist, as if reading the odds there, weighing the pins' value against making a scene with a young foreign girl. His mouth twisted into a hideous shape. He let go of my hand and spat on the sidewalk inches from my feet. Horrified, I stared for a moment at the yellow glob of mucous nearly touching my shoe. Disgusted, I spun from the man and his wares and ran off after Anne. She was waiting for me, watching from a safe distance at an incense stand, hiding behind a screen of milling fair goers.

"Anne, why'd you do that?" I demanded. I was shaking. My knees were like water.

Anne's eyes looked wild.

"Here," she said, recklessly, thrusting one of two identical brooches toward me.

They were tin pins painted gold and covered with gaudy fake diamonds.

"So classy," she crooned. "Something to remember the moment. We'll wear them forever, Ellen . . . the symbols of friendship."

6

oni yuri |
tiger lilies

Along with my friendship with Anne, two major intruders
preoccupied me during that summer. The intruders were two
men who visited Grandmother—Mr. Miyata, Grandmother's
lawyer, and Doctor Kimura, who had recently become her
physician and who, I was convinced, was trying to kill her. Mr.
Miyata lived and worked in Tokyo, flying or coming by train
whenever Grandmother summoned him, which was frequently. I'd met him in Tokyo, at Grandmother's house, and
I liked him. He had been our escort several times to the
theater and afterward had taken us out. His thick gray hair
was arranged obediently on his head. He had a pencil-thin
moustache of the same steel color. He appeared always to be
caught off-guard, as if he lived in the world of the unexpected, which he handled with competence and calm. He
seemed to love children and they him, as they had the dual
excitement of surprising him and watching him master his
surprise. Mr. Miyata dressed impeccably in dark suits in
turtle greens, earth browns, and slate and charcoal colors. He

wore startlingly white shirts, lean, striped ties, and thin socks so incredibly sheer that I wondered how he kept them lying smooth as glass on the thin legs that peered out from between the mirror-like shine of his heavy wingtip shoes and the cuffed ends of his trousers. It is curious also that he had a mustiness about him, as though he had climbed out of the same chest that housed Grandmother's old clothes, like the chiffon tea dress, frantic with yellow sunflowers, that I had worn with Sara's green heels on the previous Halloween. This subtle quality was fascinating to me. He would always knock gently on the front door, bowing graciously at the genkan, looking embarrassed and disoriented by his own presence, as though he'd materialized out of thin air without any warning. But he never arrived without Grandmother's summons, and after recovering from the initial shock of his own arrival, he would always produce some treat for the children, carefully wrapped and knotted, Japanese-style, in a purple silk scarf—dark, sweet plums, little mochi squares, or osembe crackers in different shapes, toasted golden and decorated with sesame and shiny black nori.

I felt sorry for Mr. Miyata. When Grandmother felt badly, she would call him, and when she felt worse, she would call him more frequently. He would arrive by cab from the train station, looking surprised, but unruffled. The conversation came from Grandmother's room: in conference-room whispers, she would grill him hurriedly about her financial affairs, about the sale of her Tokyo house, and he would respond earnestly, stammering sometimes, regaining control.

He'd emerge from her room with a drawn look, the small wrinkles prominent around his clear, startled eyes. Before, when Grandmother was not quite as ill, they had talked out on chairs that Ineko-san placed in the garden, the wind-teased tiger lilies bobbing about them, releasing an intoxicating fragrance. They read Tokyo newspapers together and laughed. It seemed to make Grandmother happy. But now, she was mostly in bed, the pale rose color of her bedjacket making her look paler still, the pinched wrinkle of her mouth still able to purse like a small flower or flatten against the polished ivory of her teeth. Usually, Mr. Miyata had his briefcase with him, and it, too, had that musty smell. It must have been filled with Grandmother's papers. It was just one more example of how Grandmother seemed to leave her stamp irrevocably upon him. She always slept well after he left, as if she'd just eaten, and she was pleasant and good-natured for days.

Doctor Kimura, Grandmother's physician, was a darker presence. He lived in the Big Machi and would come careening into our drive twice a week in his battered Impala, accompanied always by the same juvenile nurse who bounced about pathetically on the long, backseat of the car. Her name was Miko and she had a cringing quality, not the forthright behavior of someone like Ineko-san. Everything about her was sneaky. There was something furtive about the way she would pour Grandmother's ice water from the gray thermos pitcher at her bedside and administer a palmful of white pills or dreadful pink capsules full of crystals. She had a way of wincing at the doctor's gaze, as though he hit her. This behavior alternated with a sticky, fawning secrecy.

Dr. Kimura's car would screech over the gravel, hurling rock and dust, and slam to a stop. The doctor and his sneaky accomplice of a nurse would tumble out—the too-young doctor, always in the same shiny black suit and rumpled shirt, usually tieless, sometimes with a black rubber and steel stethoscope around his neck where the tie should have been. He seemed to move without breathing through the house, as though there'd be something damaging about doing that. I'd watch as he gulped the air hurriedly between his dirty midnight-blue Impala and our ragged front wall, sealing himself with a shudder.

Anne and I peered from our hiding place behind one of the pink sheds.

"Watch how he takes a breath," I hissed. "There. Look! And now he won't breathe the whole time."

Doctor Kimura had a face like the wax vegetables that are used in food displays in the windows of Japanese restaurants. It was frightening.

Anne drew back behind the shed, crushing herself against it, back to the wall, arms spread, palms backward on either side of her.

"Oh, God," she said, "just like Mr. Sardonicus."

This was a movie Anne had seen recently at the Japanese theater. It was an old film that starred some screwy old actor like Peter Lorrie, who Anne enjoyed imitating. I had not seen the movie, but I was familiar enough with the malevolent nature of Mr. Sardonicus from Anne's imitations. An even darker color was cast over the doctor and his solicitous nurse. I thought of my grandmother downing spoonfuls of white powder from the flat round tin they'd given her. It was only as big as her palm. She'd cough into her handkerchief until her thin brows seemed to knot over the bridge of her nose and her already fleshless cheeks looked sunken and deflated.

"He has a scar on his head. Did you see it?"

"No," Anne replied, wide-eyed and aghast.

"Yes," I said, remembering the thumb-sized lavender scar on that otherwise flawless face. "Right there." I dramatically pressed Anne's right temple. "It looks as though someone has fooled with his brain."

"Oh, God. How weird. Why does your mother let him in the house?" she asked.

"He's Grandmother's doctor," I replied matter-of-factly. "But, I think he's trying to kill her."

This was my worst fear, and now that I had shared it, I felt better. I hadn't told Sara, afraid that she would casually dismiss the idea. But Anne, my good friend and partner in espionage, who had urged me to buy my first trench coat and dump my yellow slicker in favor of Burberry brown, didn't question my suspicions. She was as intrigued as I.

"Look," I said, starting out from behind the shed, troubled by spiders that were collecting just under the roof. "Let's go find Mimi. Doctor Kimura likes her. She can give us more information."

The doctor did seem fond of Mimi. She'd accused him of tripping her once. Running past him in the hall, she'd lost her balance and went sprawling and sliding on her belly along the tatami. He had laughed his grating crow's caw of a laugh. Mimi was furious. She blamed him for her fall. She claimed he had tripped her. As a peace offering, he had given her a plastic syringe to use in water fights against Samuel and Gray's plastic pistols. This, of course, had appeased her; but she still wasn't exactly his friend.

"We'll get Mimi to spy on him," Anne suggested.

This was an excellent idea, but I was a bit irritated by the cavalier way Anne had of exposing Mimi to danger. The possibility of intrigue, however, outweighed my reluctance. We struck out across the gravel and tiptoed past the parked Impala, peering in through its dusty windows. We planned to find Mimi, but first we went to the back door, and going into the kitchen, got Ineko-san to give us a couple of cokes. We leaned on the white picket fence at the back of the house, which was giving way from kids leaning on it all the time, and surveyed the wide, uncultivated vista that stretched out from there. Dry dirt and tall weeds rimmed a criss-cross of trails cut by the boys' bikes. A naked tetherball pole stood out in the middle of the brush and the scuffed earth where Gene had planted it—a strange sentry. There was a big bald space where Gray and Samuel played baseball. Anne gave a rendition of my big-lips imitation of Mick Jagger singing, "Satisfaction." It was a beautiful, perfect late-summer moment. Then we went to find Mimi.

We caught up with her rolling around on a single old skate. She agreed readily to spy on Dr. Kimura, and went about her task with such clumsiness that the doctor, I'm sure, knew something was up. Our surveillance was hardly a secret. Anne would hurry over whenever Grandmother's doctor's appointment was scheduled and hang about looking like Mata Hari in her black stockings and her air of mystery. Our only accomplishment was to steal some powder from Grandmother's tin box. We wore our white cotton church gloves to do this, and used Sara's makeup brush to brush down everything after we'd finished. We mixed the powder with water to dissolve it. We were going to conduct tests for poison, but we were afraid to test it on ourselves or on Mimi, Samuel, or Gray. We decided at last to test it upon the rabbit, but Anne felt that this would not be an accurate test because anything could kill a rabbit, so we poured the solution out onto one of the houseplants. It neither died nor flourished, proving nothing, so we gave up on our experiments, contenting ourselves to watch my grandmother instead.

I forced myself to get used to the visits of Grandmother's doctor, frequent as they'd become, and to Grandmother's tearing cough; it sounded like a long strip of silk being ripped and ripped. At night, during that summer, when a hot stickiness kept us awake and no relief blew in through the thin mesh of the summer screens, I would hear her for what seemed like hours, my hands clutching the crisp white line of the sheet at the top of my covers, my head nearly raised from the pillow, waiting for it to stop. Even Mimi, in her bed near mine, would toss and turn. I don't know whether from the heat or Grandmother's coughing, but Mimi's dark brows soon joined in a frown, and the pout of her mouth began to form unhappy murmurs. It was not long before she started to talk in her sleep.

My sleep was also troubled. Once, I dreamed that Dr. Kimura had come with a long syringe and was trying to push it into the back of Grandmother's neck, and that Grandmother was struggling so that she became all tangled up in her bedclothes as though she were bound. Then Mimi ran up like a vicious little hound and savagely bit the doctor's leg. He tried to kick her off. I was running after Ineko-san, who was sitting sidesaddle on the farmer's plow horse. She disappeared across the fields, smiling sadly and waving her cornflower-covered handkerchief. Gene had been stuck in a box somewhere, and I didn't know where to find him. I found him, finally, in a jar in one of the cupboards, and he spoke to me from inside the jar, but I couldn't get him out, so I started to cry.

I tried to avoid the doctor, though I'd hang possessively about Grandmother's room whenever he came by. Cornered in the narrow hallway once, at his approach, unable to retreat hastily before he rounded the corner, I backed against the cool plaster of the wall. He brushed past me, smelling like medicines and death and raised an eyebrow significantly, as if we shared some secret. The suggestion of intimacy sickened me. I thought I had narrowly escaped personal contact, but the doctor stopped and spun around to address me.

"You are not like your grandmother at all," he said in English, his face arranged in a curious smile. He made it sound like an insult.

"Obachan, obasanyo neh?" I said, trying to match what I thought was his tone. "My grandmother is an old woman, you know."

"Yes," he said, his nasty smile still on his lips. "And you are no woman at all." He laughed and shrugged, quickly turning away. I felt as if I'd been slapped. My mouth hung open, any cleverness choked. That made me despise him all the more.

I could never explain this to Sara or to Grandmother, whose dependence upon him was complete. When he was with her, if the door happened to be closed, I imagined Grandmother drugged and asleep while he rifled through the cherrywood dresser, passing his hands over my things. If the door was ajar, and he caught me passing by, I would hear him make a comment to Grandmother in Japanese. I was certain he'd made a remark about me. He would lean in the doorway of Grandmother's bedroom, his black doctor's valise on the ground near his foot, talking with Grandmother, Sara, or Ineko-san, while I sat, trapped in my room at the other end of the hall, afraid to come out, afraid, almost, to breathe, while he talked on and on.

I had not given up entirely on spying. Once, through the narrow slit of the partially opened doorway, I watched him examine my grandmother. Sitting on the edge of the bed, Dr. Kimura had Grandmother bare one of her breasts. She fumbled weakly with the closures of her pajama shirt, her hands slipping on the tiny shell buttons.

"Otetsudai shimashoka. Let me help you," he whispered, leaning toward her.

His familiarity with my grandmother shocked me. I hated the thought of him touching her.

The nurse, in a white nylon dress and stockings, her back to them, conducted her business from the top of my dresser. She looked back over her shoulder, craning her neck.

The pajama shirt fell away under the doctor's hands, leaving a shoulder and one side exposed. He scooted closer toward Grandmother, lifting his stethoscope, placing the black rubber tips in his ears. Her breast drooped like a tired flower. She winced as the cold mouth of the stethoscope touched it.

"Sumi-masen, chotto seki-o-shite mite kudasai," said Dr. Kimura.

Grandmother gave two short little coughs, turning her head from him.

"Mo-ichi-do," the doctor said.

She turned her head to the other side, avoiding him, as one warding off a blow. Her mouth formed a mirror-like oval. The two coughs were forced out from behind the flat expression of her face.

"Mo-ichi-do. Again," he barely breathed.

This time the two tiny coughs were aimed directly at him, the ragged expulsion of breath hitting his forehead, ruffling the inky thickness of his hair. Again, I saw the lavender scar.

"Hi, yoroshii, kekko-desu. Good. Very good," he said.

He let his stethoscope drop, and making Grandmother turn slightly, he addressed the blank white expanse of her back, tapping the smooth wall of it curiously, like a man searching for a secret passageway in through the unmarked facade. Facing the wall, her neck bent slightly, the pajama shirt draped over one pallid shoulder, she made me think of a candle melting, the bedclothes, like tallow, pouring away from her.

The doctor's hands were massaging her shoulders and neck. He leaned closely toward her, his words low, almost in her ear. I could not hear what he said. Grandmother's head seemed to bow more deeply as he massaged. An exhausted sigh shuddered through her. Straightening, the doctor turned to his nurse who was waiting, her mouth as shapeless as an infant's, and fired his instructions at her. The nurse nearly stumbled in her haste to gather up the tray and thermos pitcher from the nightstand next to the bed. Not wanting to be caught, I almost tripped in my haste to back off from the doorway and scoot from the hall and into my room before she barrelled through the door. I heard the rattle of the tray in the kitchen, the front door, the groan and slam of the trunk of the doctor's automobile, and the clatter of a bicycle on the drive.

He must have sent her for something.

I sat in my room for a long time, listening. Then I went over to Mimi's dresser and rearranged the little stuffed bears that she kept lined up on top of it. I threw out a withered honeysuckle blossom stuck in the black swan vase that Ineko-san had given me. When I touched it, all of the petals fell onto the dresser top. I had to scoop them into the cup of my hand and throw them by the fistfuls into the trash. The other flowers in the vase shuddered and threatened to fall away too. I rearranged them, then sat on the edge of the bed, my hands folded daintily in my lap. I sat and just stared for the longest time. When I walked down the hall toward the kitchen, I had no intention of stopping at Grandmother's door.

He was leaning over her, helping her button the long line of opalescent disks that closed the pajama top. "O-tsukare-desuka?" he asked. Dr. Kimura wanted to know if she'd been especially fatigued.

"Mochiron," Grandmother replied tersely. She was irritated, and she snapped at him. I was glad. She was ill. What did he expect?

I did not care to see him fall back into the armchair or to see Grandmother sink back into her pillows with her hands over her heart. I walked stiffly to the kitchen, made a sandwich, and pouring a huge glass of milk, sat down to eat.

Dr. Kimura stepped into the kitchen. "Obachama-ni mizuo tsugimasho," he explained as he went about filling Grandmother's pitcher, which had been left by the nurse on the countertop, with ice water.

I said nothing.

"Tomodachi-wa doko?" He asked me in impolite Japanese about Anne.

"At home," I answered shortly, in English.

"Ah, so." he said slowly, raising one eyebrow, his mouth curling into the sneer he had instead of a smile.

His teeth were very white, and his lips stretched across them were a brilliant magenta.

I couldn't stand it. "Look," I said testily, pushing my chair from the table and moving toward him, "I'll take my grandmother's water to her. Why don't you just go?"

I didn't want him administering to Grandmother. I was convinced he was going to kill her.

"Oh, no," he said, holding the pitcher beyond my reach, a canine grin pulling up the corners of his mouth, turning his smooth face into a devilish mask.

"Ooooh, no" he repeated, in English.

Then he whispered something in Japanese, leered at me, and walked airily out of the kitchen.

"Give up my office as caregiver?" he laughed. "Sonna koto wa dekinaiyo," he crowed. "Oh, no. I wouldn't dream of it."

7

wampaka tachi |
the pack

The new boys were Ryan and Laird, and they had a sister, Peganne, and baby twin brothers, Bobbie and Eric. Ryan's hair was a dull brown, but Laird's, Peganne's, and that of the twins was a fiery orange. Oddly, Ryan, who had the brown hair, also had the worst temper. I once saw him nearly bust another boy's head open with a rock. Their faces and arms—anything touched by the sun—were a mass of freckles. So we told them that if they were dogs, they would be spot-covered. They were boisterous children, even more so than my brothers and sister. They ran about in a pack, herding their five shelties before them—dogs like small collies, as dusty and orange as they were.

Like most of our neighbors, they lived more than a mile away, but they seemed always to be hanging around, parading their skeleton bikes stripped of fenders and hardware, dressed in their rough dirt-caked boots and their ragged sweatshirts and jeans. They were very poor because their father spent all their money on himself. They told us that sometimes they only had popcorn for dinner. Mrs. Brynford, or Nora, as we called their mother, was very fat and always wore the same black cardigan sweater, with moth holes in the sleeves, over her plaid cotton dresses. Often, she wore white socks and a shapeless kind of shoe that looked very comfortable but was very unattractive. Her red-brown hair was long and curly. She pulled it behind her ears and gathered it in a hairstyle that Sara called a joanna. Nora had the same freckly face as her children. Mr. Brynford was thin and mean.

Laird was the oldest and tallest child and the loudest. He refused to acknowledge the dogs that followed him devotedly. Ryan was left to care for them. Laird was older than any of the other children in the area, including me. He was continually on the perimeter of all the activities, taunting the others, squinting his eyes, and hissing "eh, chikahn," which was his way of calling someone a coward. He needed braces because his front teeth stuck straight out, but his parents were too poor to get them for him.

Peganne was also a ruffian, a lot like her brothers, around six years old, but pudgy—with a tendency to whine, which made Mimi desert her after a few weeks. Among all the children, and Samuel, Mimi, and Gray, Ryan and Gray got along the best. But every few weeks, they would fight savagely, and Gray would have a cut on his forehead or a new bruise to add to the long procession of black eyes acquired from standing in the way of Samuel's fastball.

Sara took Nora under her wing, and for months Nora came over for coffee and chatted. Sara must have been horribly bored in that place. Our old clothes disappeared and reappeared, miraculously, on the backs of the younger Brynfords. I think Ryan, Peganne, and the twins were always a little ashamed about that. Nora shared all her secrets with Sara, and these became dinner conversation, accompanied by concerned clucking and sighs of "poor Nora." Gene generally scowled, retorting that Markham Brynford was a very selfish man, implying that his family, Nora and the children, would be better off without him. Sara always ended the conversation with "and all those dogs," as if this encompassed the ultimate evil. I would think, cautiously, of Soft and how much more appropriate it was to have only one.

"All those dogs."

Everyone within the twenty square miles of Europeans and Americans that sparsely inhabited our area had dogs. But of all of these, Mr. Nielson rose above the rest, like a god on a pedestal. Mr. Nielson, an engineer, and a good friend of Gene's, raised Akitas as a hobby. He was a gray-haired American with a young Japanese wife, and his dogs were the talk of the province. An Akita is a large dog that resembles a German Shepherd in stature and form, but a Mastiff in face and bulk. It is an imposing dog. It can be trained to be vicious, but is, for the most part, of the same disposition as a Saint Bernard. In other words, these are incredible dogs, much admired by children and adults alike. Mr. Nielson had a compound where he bred them, and many had won shows. Gene said that the air base inquired often of Mr. Nielson about training his dogs as attack and guard animals, and had even purchased a few, but Mr. Nielson's best dogs were for show. I imagine, had we not acquired Soft, that we would have been the proud owners of a Nielson Akita, though Sara swore that those dogs could "go wild." She, Grandmother, and Ineko-san thought that they were responsible for the holes near the rabbit hutch. In fact, rabbits and other small animals were much despised by Mr. Nielson. He once had to put down a dog that had killed once and continued to kill until it had to be shot. Gene said Mr. Nielson was bitter about having to shoot it. His dogs, therefore, remained in their chicken wire compound. They were only taken out for exercise. Mr. Nielson always walked them on the breathtakingly regal velvet leashes that he used for his shows. Sometimes he'd need someone to walk the dogs for him. Children vied for this honor.

There was one other boy in the area worth mentioning. His name was David Vintner. He was not much approved of by parents in general. Anne and I both had crushes on him. David's mother was French and his father American. He was an engineer who worked on projects like Gene's. Sara said David's father had deserted them.

"That David," Sara would sigh, "is a juvenile delinquent. He has no supervision." This only made David more attractive to us.

David lived less than a mile from our house and had a younger sister, Claire. Claire, who was seven, wore red boots year-round. Her blue eyes were pretty, but empty. David was famous among the children in our area for taking Claire into the sunflower field when the stalks were far higher than a child could reach, undressing her, and charging admission for the boys to look at her. Claire, we had heard, was extremely compliant. David's mother could not control her children, and because of this was not well-respected by the other mothers in the area. Samuel, Mimi, and Gray were on excellent terms with David, but I avoided him precisely because of those quirky habits that had earned him his reputation.

Those quirky habits were also the reason David intrigued Anne and me. In fact, we had invented a game that centered around him. In this game, we created scenarios in which one of us was trapped, alone, with David Vintner.

"What if you were trapped on a desert island with David Vintner?" Anne asked one night at my house, initiating our favorite fantasy.

Anne, who was spending the night, was sitting up in Mimi's bed. Mimi had been temporarily moved to a sleeping bag on the floor in Samuel and Gray's room. We had to bribe her to leave. We had promised to be her slaves at some future date. Mimi was probably already sleeping blissfully in her cartoon-lined cotton cocoon in the boys' room, dreaming about that rosy event in the future. Anne and I were quite pleased with the deal. We had no intention of ever keeping our end of the bargain.

Anne had surrounded herself with magazines, comic books, hairbands, combs, and the crumbs from a package of shrimp chips that she had devoured. Her slovenly habits reminded me somewhat of Mimi. She looked quite Mimi-like amid her mess. The bedroom was perfumed with the fishy fragrance of the styrofoam-textured snacks.

"Those things stink," I said dryly.

"I like them," Anne answered, taking a deep swig from a gray-green bottle of coke. She enjoyed letting the coke dissolve the shrimp chips in her mouth. "Can you imagine?" Anne continued, the coke bottle hovering inches from her lips. "He'd force you to have his babies."

"Have sex," I corrected.

"Yes," Anne affirmed. She took another big swallow of coke.

It was perfect. I had a surprise for Anne, one that I knew would excite her. I was ready, at last, to reveal it. The slumber party had been only a pretext.

"Listen, Anne," I said warily. "I have some interesting information."

"What?" Anne asked.

"Well, it involves David Vintner."

"Really?" Anne's posture made a sudden and dramatic improvement.

"Yes," I continued. "I happen to know that Samuel and Gray have been invited by David Vintner to the sunflower field where he gets Claire to remove all of her clothes."

"You're kidding," Anne laughed. "That's great. How'd you find out?"

"From Mimi," I answered. "She wanted to go too, but they wouldn't let her. I think she's planning to follow them."

"Oh, let's follow Mimi!" Anne exclaimed.

"Yes, that's my idea." I agreed. "We'll watch Mimi tomorrow and when she sets off, we'll be behind her."

A big grin spread over Anne's face.

"Do you really think it's true, that he really makes Claire take off her clothes?"

"I don't know," I replied. "But we'll find out tomorrow."

"Yes, tomorrow," Anne echoed.

Summer, so far, had been pretty dull. We both hoped it was true about David and Claire.

It was late August, one of the hottest days of the year. The boys left the house in the morning. Mimi, intending to follow them, trailed behind them pedaling along one of the bumpy dirt paths into the sunflower field to where David had set up his sideshow. Anne and I watched her leave.

"I think it's time to track her," said Anne. "Do you know where she's headed?"

"I think so," I answered.

We took the same path that Mimi had—out into the sunflower field. It was hot, the air full of gnats.

Seven-foot sunflowers towered in rows—a thick, hempy jungle. The ground around them was lumpy and hard. We found Mimi's bike in a pile with others not far from the path. Anne and I inched along, trying to slip soundlessly through the tall, drying stalks. Screened by the ragged foliage, less than twelve feet away, we heard voices.

"She has to pay too." It was David Vintner's voice.

"Why? She's a girl." Samuel's voice rose in hot debate.

"I don't care, Sam. Mimi still has to pay. If she doesn't pay, no one can see."

Samuel lowered his voice. "Mimi," he said, "Do you have any yen? You need ninety yen. That's about forty cents."

"No, Sam," Mimi answered. "But I have a quarter at home."

"Okay," Samuel said gently.

"Did you hear that David? Mimi can give you a quarter."

"Well, all right," David reluctantly agreed. "Since you're a girl, Mimi, I'll take the quarter. I guess this is nothing new to you. Come here, Claire," he commanded.

Anne and I crawled the twelve feet up to the voices. We peeked in past the jungle of fat, furry stalks.

The three boys and Mimi stood in a crescent. Into the center of this half-moon stepped Claire, the star of the show, wearing nothing but a dopey look and her little red boots. Claire looked ridiculous with her plump parts exposed.

Anne and I were just getting ready to crash through the sunflower stalks when Laird Brynford appeared on the opposite side of the clearing, freckled arms bulging from the sweatshirt from which he'd removed the sleeves.

"Hey, how come you didn't invite me, David?" he jeered, breaking through the circle of children.

David was not rattled at all.

"Because, I'd like to think you've seen naked girls before," he said calmly. "And I doubt if you have any money."

Laird Brynford was insulted. He scrunched up his face so his freckles made one big brown mask and his teeth stuck out like a chipmunk's.

"I have money," Laird said testily, throwing a few paltry coins down into the dirt. "I have money. I think it's pretty nasty to sell your sister, you know. That's pretty sleezy, Vintner."

"Claire doesn't mind," David answered.

"Yeah, well good. You like this, huh, Claire? Yeah, aren't you a cutie?"

Laird lunged at Claire and roughly grabbed one of her arms. Claire's face filled with terror.

"Let her go Brynford," David hissed. "Nobody touches Claire."

"You mean no one but you," Laird laughed, his hands moving all over Claire's body. "I paid my money," he said, "and looking ain't worth what I paid." He pawed Claire some more. She was like a little rag doll being thrown about, not resisting.

David aimed a roundhouse punch directly at Laird Brynford's jaw. Laird let Claire go. He managed to side-step quickly, avoiding the blow. But David was already poised to deliver another one.

I grabbed Anne's arm. We broke into the clearing.

"Ellen!" David Vintner was shocked.

"David, I can't believe you," I scolded.

Anne gathered Claire's clothes and thrust them toward her. She was embarrassed and started to cry.

"You should have done that before you took off your clothes," Anne said meanly.

Mimi was hiding behind her long bangs, watching me closely. I said, "Mimi, go home."

"You're not going to tell, are you, Ellen?" Gray asked shakily.

"Maybe we are," Anne threatened.

"If anyone finds out about this, you're dead, Laird." I said.

We were about to find out how true that was. I don't know how many people Mimi had told. She'd told Peganne, for sure, who leaked the information to Laird. Peganne also told Markham Brynford, her father.

Markham Brynford had been hunting that whole morning for Laird. He hadn't found him. He had followed the kids' path down into the sunflower field. I don't know how long he'd been at the spot. Not long, I suspected. Mr. Brynford was the kind of man who used his fists first and never asked questions. He saw us all standing there in the clearing rimmed by the fierce yellow sunflowers. He saw Claire, standing naked, and he saw his son, Laird. I don't think he noticed Claire's tears or the shock on our faces. I think all he saw was his big, buck-toothed boy and the rage climbed up like a red tide and filled him.

First he flew at Laird with his hands, hard as thin blocks of wood, chopping at one side of his face, then the other. Laird reeled from the blows, his head snapped back and forth, as if his neck were made of elastic.

"What are you doing here, huh?" Markham Brynford growled through clenched teeth. "You're nothing but trouble. You're the worst scum around, you punk."

Then Brynford punched his son in the gut. This brought Laird to his knees. Brynford kicked him, hard, in the chest. He was wearing big army boots, the kind that one day, when they were too worn for him to wear, he'd hand down to Laird. Laird hit the dust. We scattered. Then, Mr. Brynford delivered a series of kicks. Laird couldn't get up. He just lay there in the dirt and his father kept kicking him, shouting "punk" each time his boots pounded into Laird's body.

None of us knew what to do. We just watched while Markham Brynford spent his fury on his son. Then he reached down and hauled Laird up by his arm, grabbing it under the shoulder and pulling it so roughly we thought he was going to dislocate the limb.

"You're coming home with me," he snarled. "I ain't finished with you. I'll teach you to shame me," he said.

"And you," he said viciously, turning to David Vintner. "I know your Mama can't do anything with you. I won't even say what I think is wrong with her. Stay away from my children. Stay away from my boys," he said menacingly. He looked at each one of us, tacking our faces up in his mind like wanted posters. "You kids get out of here," he hollered. "You hear me? You kids get out of here, now."

Then he left with Laird.

We'd been too paralyzed to move even a muscle. But when Markham Brynford left, we scattered like crows. Anne and I ran off, leaving David and Claire. Mimi and the boys grabbed their bikes.

"Hey, Mimi, don't forget, you owe me a quarter," David called after them from the field as they pedaled furiously away.

namako

sea cucumber

なまこ

8

koji |
orphans

It was mean Markham Brynford's fault that the orphans came into our lives.

One chilly September morning, Nora Brynford came to our door, arms full of the old clothes Sara had given her for her boys and Peganne.

"Sara," she said, looking down at her funny-shaped shoes, "I'm giving these back. Markham says we don't want to take cast-offs. I thank you Sara, but you know Markham. He's just too proud."

Nora handed over the clothing she'd folded and bundled so neatly and left, her head bent, her old coat layered over her moth-eaten sweater, picking her way up the gravel drive, back to the rutted dirt road that led away from our house.

The return of our old clothes plunged Sara into an odd depression. She shook her head sadly and sighed when Nora walked off. That sighing seemed to continue for weeks.

"How can people ignore the physical needs of children?" she asked Gene unexpectedly one evening as we sat at dinner.

Our plates were heaped high with lamb chops and rice. I thought of the Brynfords at dinner, and how they sometimes only had popcorn. "Popcorn and peanut butter," Peganne had disclosed, as if she were sharing some valuable secret about the inner life of her family. They weren't really that poor. It was just that Mr. Brynford spent all of their money on himself.

"I don't know, Sara," Gene replied. "I guess some people just think children don't matter."

"Hmmm," Sara responded, lapsing into despondent silence.

Samuel, Mimi, Gray, and I exchanged worried glances. We hadn't told Sara or Gene about the incident in the sunflower field. We wondered what they would have done if they'd seen Markham Brynford beating up on Laird.

Sara liked giving to others. When she was a small girl in Shanghai, she gave all her toys away to the children that begged in the city streets. "Street urchins," she called them, adding proudly, "they were my friends." Sara told us that she would come home from her boarding school for the holidays to a Christmas tree surrounded by presents. By January, when she returned to school, not a gift was left in the house. Grandmother let Sara know that she felt it was thoughtless and frivolous to give away all her gifts, but she continued to buy them for Sara every year, and Sara continued to hand them out to the first poor children she could find.

Sometimes Sara even gave our things away without asking. Once she gave away all of Mimi's old stuffed toys to a dirty, blonde neighborhood child. We discovered this when we found Mimi's battered, black-and-white bunny in a mud puddle far from the house. I brought it home and told Mimi that she had to take better care of her toys, but Mimi knew nothing about it. That's how we discovered what Sara had done. It wasn't so bad that Sara had given the old toys away; Mimi didn't play with them anymore. But, the child that she'd given them to was dirty and careless. Mimi would have nothing to do with this girl even before she had mistreated one of Mimi's favorite stuffed animals. Mimi was furious with Sara for days.

I thought it was probably a good thing that Grandmother was leaving Akishima to her brothers instead of to Sara. Sara most likely would have given that away, too.

So Sara was moping about those old clothes and mourning their return when Ineko-san mentioned the orphanage in Hokkaido. She was trying to be helpful, of course, but she made things much worse.

Hokkaido is the wild, almost-forgotten island just north of Honshu. Floating between the Sea of Okhosk and the Sea of Japan, it is linked to Honshu by ferry across the gray Tsugaru Straits.

The Hokkaido orphanage was a small one, run by a handful of Japanese nuns who took care of around twenty parentless children. They had no source of support except their own labor and the meager contributions provided by the region's scant population. Ineko-san had a brother who lived and farmed in Hokkaido. Through him she discovered the orphans. Every year, she gave them rabbits, vegetables, fish, and whatever extra clothing she could spare. She told Sara that the orphans could really use our old clothing. The Hokkaido winters were cold, and the next one was fast on its way.

Ineko-san's suggestion had an amazing effect on Sara.

"Oh," Sara exclaimed, "yes, Hokkaido. I've been to Hokkaido. We went there one summer when I was a child. That is the land of the Ainu."

The Ainu, Sara told us, were the original inhabitants of Japan. They had blue eyes, wore little clothing, and were covered with hair. The Ainu lived in Hokkaido's deep, primal forests, in communities high in the mountains and in villages along the cold coast.

"They are far more Russian than Japanese," Sara continued. "They keep history alive through their oral tradition. They are the tellers of marvelous stories."

Naturally, based on Sara's account, we wanted to go to Hokkaido. We expected a wonderland full of magical Ainu, but it wasn't like that at all.

Hokkaido was a desolate place. Volcanic peaks, coarse and craggy like brutal stalagmites climbed into the cold gray sky. Along the lonely coastline, thin cranes flapped along with long necks like matchsticks and heads capped in a fiery, sulfurous red.

We all went together on that first orphanage visit. Our crossing over the Tsugaru Straits was rough. We had to wear heavy coats to keep out the damp, clammy hands of the fog. The roads went from gravel to dirt to mud and sometimes to almost no road at all. Most of the landscape was unfarmed and untamed; where farms did exist, they were of the most primitive kind—mud huts or shacks with rickety tools scattered or hung about them.

The orphanage, at the end of a mire-clogged road, must have once been a farmhouse. It was made of straw-filled mud and the roof was thatch. Looking like wings, a couple of barracks-like buildings with tin roofs butted up against it on either side, giving the orphanage a cruciform shape. One wing served as the dormitory, the other as the refectory.

We got there at noon, later than we had planned. The nuns gave Gene and Sara a hurried but courteous welcome, then ushered us into the dining hall to have lunch with the orphans. When we entered the lunchroom, one extremely thin little boy rushed up to Sara and grabbed her hand.

"Okasan?" he asked, desperately pulling at her.

"No, not your mother," the shortest Japanese nun said kindly, bending down to the small child and gently prying his hand loose.

"Come now, let us have lunch," she said.

He trotted obediently beside her, looking plaintively back over his shoulder at Sara, the question of "mother?" still in his eyes. Sara's mouth hung open, still formed around the "yes," she wanted to say but did not.

"He does that with every woman who comes in the door," the other nun said apologetically. "He's been here for months. His mother is dead, but he thinks she is coming to get him."

Sara looked very sad.

We sat down to a lunch of white rice and chicken and various kinds of fish. I noticed the orphans ate rice and vegetables—mainly turnips and carrots. They were the thick, tough kind of carrots—the kind we usually gave to Mimi's rabbit.

"Why don't you tell that boy that his mother is dead?" I asked the nun who'd stayed with us.

"We've tried to tell him his mother wasn't coming," she said.

"But you didn't actually tell him?" I demanded.

Sara's eyes looked as if she were suffering. "Ellen," she said, "that's enough."

"Well, I'd tell him," I said. "I'd tell him she's dead, and she'll never come. I wouldn't let him go on hoping for something that won't happen. It's ridiculous," I added frostily. "It's worse. It's pathetic."

It seemed cruel to let the boy continue to believe that each woman to walk in the door might be his mother. It seemed to me that the most horribly hopeless thing was his hope.

"I'd tell him," I repeated. "I'd tell him the truth."

I visited the orphanage three times after that with Sara, and that little boy always ran up and ambushed her with the same pitiful question. Then finally, one visit, he was not there to greet us with his wretched little wishes. Sara said nothing, but I watched her eyes move like silent sentinels over the haggard young faces that surrounded us, searching the rows of children for him. Sara was afraid to ask where he was, but I wasn't.

"Oh, it's so very sad," the nun murmured in response. He got sick, and he never got better. He grew weaker and weaker. I'm so sorry. He's dead."

"That's what happens when you feed someone lies," I said hotly. I thought of the orphan waking every morning with the hope that his mother would come for him. What must he have felt as each day unraveled into the next? What does it feel like to lose hope piece by piece, without explanation, until there is nothing left?

I knew it was wrong not to say anything. But I never did tell him the truth. I never screamed, "Stop it. Stop it," when he attached himself to us. "This is Sara. She isn't your mother. Don't you know your mother is dead? She's not going to come." And Sara never said anything either. No, we never slammed him brutally in the face with the truth to save him from the heartbreaking disappointment that his hope brought him to, over and over again. Instead, we let him believe, so that we could pretend that his mother was still alive. That made me think we were cowards.

9

namako |
sea cucumber

Splack.

  . . . splack.

  . . . splack.

Anne was a silhouette in front of the sun-smeared windowpane of the biology lab of the American school. Outside, the snow was piled high. She stood on a box, holding negatives up to the light, loudly snapping her gum.

"Ummm, these are pretty weird."

Splack.

"The inside of a frog testicle."

Splack . . . splack.

"Wow, urine crystals."

She was looking at our biology slides, and wasn't concentrating on how she put them back into their tray. She was getting them all messed up. We were alone in the spotless, clinical brilliance of the science lab at the American school—Anne and me and my squid.

"The older kids get to do frogs," Anne had drawled disdainfully during class earlier in the day as she poked at one of the squid in the shallow pan on the table.

Mr. Graham, our biology teacher, had shot her a look of annoyance. I figured, as seventh graders, we were fortunate to even have squid, though I had not liked making an incision into the rubbery yellow skin. I'd done exactly what Mr. Graham told us not to do. I'd broken the ink sack. A watery blackness had swelled and flooded the oblong cavity revealed by my incision, immersing the tiny substructures that I was supposed to draw in shadow.

With Mr. Graham's permission, I was staying late, trying to finish my drawing. I had another motive, too, for working late in the lab, which I planned to share with Anne. I looked over at her. She was jamming a few of the slides haphazardly into their plastic container.

"Anne, quit making a mess," I complained.

Anne hopped down off the box. She crammed the remaining slides thoughtlessly back into the tray. She crossed the room slowly, dragging her index finger along the lab tables and walked up to the blackboard. It was filmed with dull, yellow chalk dust. Anne pressed one side of her curled fist onto the dusty board. Then she walked along, pressing the chalk-covered side of her hand onto the slate-gray surface of the tables—once, twice, three, four times—making a tightly curled imprint, repeating "embryo, embryo, embryo" in a self-absorbed sing-song each time she made a mark on them.

I tried to ignore her, attempting to complete my picture of the squid.

"How long are you going to draw that smelly thing?" she asked with distaste.

At her approach, I was surrounded by the sudden muskiness of the gym class I'd missed that day. Anne hadn't taken a shower. We both hated our PE class. But most of all, we hated the showers Miss Ibsen tried to make us take. It had been bad enough at Mercy-Mary Catholic. There, the nuns made us wear green cotton shifts in the showers after gym class, even though the shower stalls were private. That seemed very queer to us, but it made the communal showers at the American school, full of loud naked girls, even more horrible. Most of the girls were older and more developed than we were. We felt like babies. We missed the secrecy of our Catholic school. We did our best to avoid the showers.

The lab was thick with the rotten smell of formaldehyde. This mingled with Anne's faint muskiness into a sour perfume. It made my head ache.

"This place stinks, Ellen," Anne said, echoing my thoughts. "Let's go."

"Wait," I insisted, "I'm not quite finished. Besides," I said cagily, trying to coax her into some semblance of patience, "I have something special to show you." I arranged my face into what I hoped was an enigmatic expression.

Anne paused, intrigued. "Really?" she asked. Her eyes narrowed.

I nodded, pressing hard on my pencil. I had to complete the stupid squid drawing. It was the ugliest thing in my biology notebook, a notebook otherwise full of beautiful illustrations. Of all my classes, biology was my favorite. I was fascinated with the animal kingdom—with sponges and roundworms, with mollusks and reptiles. Mr. Graham was an expert on all these things, and he shared his knowledge unstintingly. Earlier in the week, we had seen a film on the great white shark. We watched it devour a seal.

"They are a primitive and successful life form," Mr. Graham had observed. "Their DNA is set to survival. They are predators, at the top of their food chain. Emotions like love and sympathy have no place in a shark's world. It is a world of survival. Theirs is a life free of sentiment—the only mandate: to live and reproduce to ensure the continuation of their kind."

As we sat watching the great white sharks glide through blurry turquoise waters, I thought of my grandmother. She reminded me of a shark—without sentiment and relentless, programmed for survival. I drew a beautiful shark in my notebook. This notebook was one of my masterpieces. In it I had drawn amoebas, paramecia, nematodes and coelenterates; I had painstakingly depicted the life cycle of a fluke from sheep's stomach to human liver; and I had illustrated, to perfection, the digestive system of a crayfish and embellished reports on hagfish and lampreys with pictures cut from an outdated set of encyclopedias of their "rasping mouths." I finished the squid picture, hastily sketching in odd curlicues and inventing entrails to fill the empty cavity. I was irritated about having to do this. But Anne was never one to wait patiently.

"Done," I announced, closing the notebook.

"Finally," Anne grumbled. Then she paused significantly, waiting for me to reveal the promised surprise.

I rummaged about in my book bag and produced a small key. Anne's eyes darted to the gray row of metal lockers that banked the back wall of the lab. A big grin spread appreciatively above the sly point of her chin.

"You stole the key!" she exclaimed, her brown eyes wide with admiration.

"No, I didn't," I said. "Mr. Graham gave it to me."

Anne looked suspicious and a little jealous. The lockers in the back of the room housed Mr. Graham's private collection of biology specimens. They were rarely opened, and then, only in Mr. Graham's presence. I know Anne didn't believe that he had just given me the key, but I didn't care to explain to her how I got it.

A few days before when Mr. Graham had handed back our biology notebooks, I flushed when I saw the big red "A++" written inside the front cover of mine. That day, he asked me to stay after class, which I did, waiting patiently while everyone else filed out of the room. I sat on one of the high stools, my hands folded on the table before me. He stood a few yards away, behind the stainless steel sink in the deserted lab, fidgeting with his pen. He walked over to the stool where I was seated. In his hands he clutched a magazine which he rolled and unrolled. He seemed to be very nervous. He was making me nervous.

"You know, Ellen," he said, rolling and unrolling his magazine, "you are an excellent artist."

"Thank you," I replied, pleased by his praise.

"What amazes me," he continued, "is how well—excuse me—how meticulously you commit what you see to paper. Every detail has value. Nothing is left unexposed."

I didn't know what he was getting at, so I said "thank you" again, and smiled. I noticed, then, when he was standing close to me, that he had little wrinkles around his green eyes, a spatter of freckles on his forehead and that his hair was very thin. I could draw him, I thought.

The biology lab was sunny and bright. I was warmed by his flattery. My smile must have encouraged him, because he came a little closer. I could smell the flat nicotine pall of his last cigarette.

"I was sort of wondering if you could draw something like this," he asked. His voice had become dry and edgy, like a couple of cracked leaves chapping against one another. He opened the magazine to a particular page. He hastily shoved it in front of me. I noticed the nicotine stain on his middle finger. He had bitten off some of his nails in an irregular fashion.

I took the magazine picture and looked at it. It was a picture of a near-naked woman. She had puffy, blonde hair. She was leaning back on a leopard-skin couch and wearing a pair of fur-covered panties. Her underpants looked like the mink collar on my favorite red coat, the one I'd torn jumping off a chain-link fence the winter before. This woman was not wearing anything but the panties, and she had the biggest breasts I had ever seen in my life. My guess was that they were the size of pumpkins, and she was holding them as if she wanted someone to take a big bite, as though they were terribly heavy. I thought they really must be. I'd never seen anything like them. I don't think I said anything. I just stared, my jaw fallen, amazed by those enormous breasts. Mr. Graham was watching me. He took a long drag from a cigarette he'd lit and blew out, encircling my head in a torn veil of smoke.

"Do you think you could draw that?" he asked slowly, all of his nervousness gone.

I looked up, startled to find myself pinned by a pair of brittle-bright irises.

"Yes, I think so," I stammered, still overwhelmed by the breasts.

"Yes," he whispered, "I thought so. I'd like you to draw that for me. Do you think you can do that?"

He sidled up closer, looking over my shoulder at the picture in front of me. "Of course, if you do that for me, I will give you something," he said thoughtfully. "I'm sure I have something you want."

He drew one ragged-nailed finger up my arm. I could feel his breath on the top of my head.

"Okay," I said, thinking quickly and at the same time almost not thinking. "Yes. Yes, you have something I want."

That is how I acquired the key.

Anne and I addressed the lockers in the back of the room. They were regular school lockers—the kind students keep their books in—all closed with big padlocks. There were three parallel vents at eye level in each of the doors. From these vents seeped, malignantly, the oppressive odor of formaldehyde that tented the room and made it somber in spite of the large, sun-filled windows. The lockers stood like long, sad coffins presiding over the back of the lab. They held Mr. Graham's treasured specimens—large glass jars in which anemones, roundworms, organs, even—most horrifying of all—a fetus, floated sorrowfully. The jars were sealed tightly, but no lid could contain the thick smell of stalled decomposition that leaked into the air. One key unlocked all of the cabinets. We opened each one cautiously, the fetid air from the sealed interiors rushing out at us. When we had them all open, we stood back in silence, and stared, with a mixture of reverence and horror, at the rows of dark jars. Their bloated occupants hung motionless like freaks at a mournful carnival.

"My God," Anne gasped in a hushed voice, the way she mumbled her "mea culpas" in church, so that I could almost see her there, sitting beside me, her large eyes fixed on the priest's vestmented back or the elevated Eucharist. She also gossiped, in church, with the same breathless intensity, our petty rumors and stories somehow sanctified by the setting and tone.

We walked slowly up to the lockers and peered into the glass receptacles that gleamed, even in the shadowy cave of the cabinets. In one container, a pouchy, yellow-green stomach was folded upon itself, the thick wrinkles forming a face that seemed to smile at us. We searched for the fetus and when we found it, or thought we had, we could not bring ourselves to look at it, feeling somehow ashamed. Anne traced the shape of one of the jars with the tips of two tapered fingers, as if she were trying to feel through the glass, her soft eyebrows puckered into a frown. We moved carefully from cabinet to cabinet, agape, like children enthralled by a sideshow.

I took a deep breath, trying to break away from the heavy shroud of formaldehyde that pulled at us. I walked over to the windows. The late sun had cast them in bright topaz. I picked up the box that Anne had been standing on earlier.

"I'm going to draw one of these," I said, scrupulously positioning the box at the foot of one of the lockers. I had to stand on tiptoe to reach the particular jar. I climbed down cautiously, mindful not to slip or drop it. I had selected it long ago when it had made a brief appearance during a lecture on coelenterates. It was my favorite creature. The jar seemed to have a life of its own. It threatened to slide from my hands. I walked over to one of the lab tables and set the glass container on top of it, surprised that the hand that had gripped it was not wet. Had I imagined a wetness? Only the dull smell of formaldehyde lingered on my fingers and on the flat of my palm.

The brown thing in the jar looked like a long pouch fringed at the mouth with whisker-like tentacles.

"This is a sea cucumber," I said. "It is an animal. Doesn't it look a lot like a vegetable, though? It's even named for a vegetable. It must be horrible to be so strange that nobody knows what you really are."

Anne leaned close to the jar in which the cucumber dangled quiescently, so close that her long lashes appeared to brush the glass. Next to the embalmed form, her face looked pale, like a small moon. "It's so awful looking," she murmured again with the hushed appreciation generally reserved for only the holiest things in church. "What are you going to do with it?"

"I'm taking it home with me," I reported with great satisfaction. "Mr. Graham told me I could."

Anne looked up quizzically, and then back at the jar, as though she were trying to draw some connection. I offered no explanations. I wrapped the jar in my woolen, navy blue sweater and slid it into my bag. We didn't say much on the way home. Anne surprised me by getting off the bus at my stop.

"I'm walking to your house with you," she declared.

The dry snow crunched under our boots. It looked like dirty lace trimming the sides of the road.

"Are you going to show that to anyone else?" Anne asked suddenly. She had on a pair of green earmuffs, that, along with her big dark eyes, made her look especially childish.

"Yes. I'm going to show it to Sara. I think she will like it. Don't you think I should?"

Anne nodded. "Yeah, I guess so."

She smiled weakly. We had reached the drive of my house. The icy gravel grumbled beneath our feet as we marched along under the fiberglass roof of the carport. Suddenly, the melting snow and the fading light of the late January sun struck me as terribly sad.

"I think it will make quite an impact," I bragged.

"Yes, it will," Anne agreed. "It's amazing. You are amazing," she added. Then, unexpectedly, she threw her arms around me, kissed me hard on the forehead, and ran noisily up the drive to the snowy bank of the road, her short coat flapping around her. Her kiss on my forehead remained a syrupy, hot imprint.

I knew as I entered the genkan and took off my shoes that something was wrong. Gene was home. He stood in the kitchen, leaning against one of the counters. I thought he would get the neat white sleeve of his shirt dirty on the usually sticky surface. Ineko-san was standing in one corner of the kitchen, sniffing into a handkerchief that she held up to her nose and mouth. Sara sat in one of the kitchen chairs, her back straight as a rod, her face colorless.

"I'm home," I announced hopefully, as though I expected this would somehow break the spell under which they seemed frozen. Sara turned her head and stared at me as if she couldn't quite place me.

Gene said, "Ellen, your grandmother has had a stroke. The doctor's just been here."

Ineko-san sniffed loudly in her corner of the room. I noticed the faint smell of disinfectant and medication that was Dr. Kimura's signature.

"Is she all right?" I asked feeling my plan to surprise Sara crumble. Selfishly, I wanted Grandmother to be fine so that

Gene could go back to work and Sara would get out of that chair and Ineko-san would stop her sniveling and I could show Sara the sea cucumber.

Gene said, "The doctor says she's doing all right. Ineko-san will be staying; I'll need you to help her out."

"Okay," I said simply. I went and stood next to Sara, my arms wrapped protectively around my book bag.

I wanted to pull out the sea cucumber and show it to her. I imagined her face filling with wonder. She'd like it. She would be profoundly amazed. It was my little creature. I'd found something as strange as anything Sara had known. Instead, I did nothing. Sara reached up and pushed back the hair that had settled across my forehead. The movement had a mechanical quality, as though she had brushed at a moth.

"There's a good child," she said tonelessly. "Your grandmother's very ill, Ellen. Why don't you go look in on her?"

"All right, Sara, I will," I responded and fled from the room. I fled from the people frozen there, from the meticulous knot of Gene's tie, from Ineko-san's crumpled white handkerchief, from the loose fitting platinum rings on Sara's left hand.

The metal doorknob was icy. Grandmother's room was icy as well. It was like walking into a refrigerator. The heavy curtains were drawn. Puffs of mist seemed to form with my breath. The smell of medication assailed me. Grandmother lay on the bed under a thick shell of patterned silk coverlets. Her face, helmeted with steely-gray hair, was barely visible at the head of the bed, and her thin, bed-jacketed arms stretched on either side of her on top of the heavy futons, so that she looked like a pharaoh or the top of a marble sarcophagus. Her breathing was shallow, her face motionless—a mask—the flesh of her body draped so sparely over her bones that I thought I could almost see through it to the bed beneath her. The frigid air of the room scratched at my throat and lungs when I breathed. I felt it was cold enough to make my nose bleed. Unable to stand it, I wanted to leave. Then Grandmother's eyes opened, depthless, like two broken bits of black glass. Her mouth pulled at the corners stretching her thin lips across her teeth as if she were trying to speak, and her gaze moved down toward her hand. It was opening and closing stiffly and the effort was making her arm shake. She seemed to want something, but I wasn't sure what. Fearfully, I put my own hand in hers, and when her fingers closed around mine, the strength of her grip frightened me. Her hand was cold, like the room, like the silk covers beneath it. Suddenly, I realized that my hand was locked in a vice. Grandmother's hand was not going to open. I was trapped. Then her eyes closed, and I stood beside her for a long time staring into the lineless map of her face.

"What do you want from me?" I asked the face of the demanding old woman who was so acutely critical, who thought that I had no soul. Then I asked it in Japanese.

All around me, playing hide and seek in the silence, were whispering voices. "What do you want? What do you want?" they echoed like gossips mocking me over a fence. "She doesn't know. No one will tell her," they tittered. The voices grew louder and louder. I wanted to put my hands over my ears, but Grandmother's fingers were still gripping mine. I felt dizzy. It was as if I'd ascended to an enormous height and the air was so thin that I could not get enough. I felt hollow and light-headed. I could no longer feel my body.

This must be what a ghost feels like, I thought, as the world started spinning and consciousness seemed to start to slip out from under me. Then I heard my grandmother's breathing cutting through the low buzz of the voices. In and out, in and out, in long, muffled rasps, like a door creaking open and shut, pulling me back to the bedroom. I let it bring me back to the bedside, let myself be soothed by the laboring saw of her breath. Then the voices subsided and Grandmother's hold on me loosened a bit so I could pry my hand free.

I walked shakily to the window and peered through the curtains that she kept perpetually drawn. The last droopy daylight was eking away. Then, I tiptoed from the room, closing the door behind me, my footsteps soundless in the tatami hallway.

The rest of the house was silent too. In my empty room, I opened my book bag and eased out the jar containing the sea cucumber, unwinding the sweater I'd wrapped around it. Sitting cross-legged on my bed, I studied the specimen. I turned it around and around. The sea cucumber bobbed sadly in its mordant bath. I imagined it must have floated somewhere at the bottom of the sea like that, passive and silent, like something asleep. Or maybe when it was alive, it had moved, finding its way across the slimy ocean floor, eating and thinking and dreaming the way all animals do. It didn't seem right for living things to pass silently from existence with their secrets still locked up inside them. Grandmother was like that. So was Sara. And in a way, I was just like that too. Suddenly I wanted to smash the glass against the wall of my bedroom, releasing the thing from its prison of pickling liquor. Instead, I sat helplessly on my bed, clutching the jar's flawless surface.

10

deshi |
apprentice

"How is your grandmother?" Mr. Graham asked.

"Oh, she's better," I said. "It was just a mild stroke."

Grandmother was recovering under Dr. Kimura's care, regaining shaky ground.

"And do you still think the doctor is trying to kill her?"

"I know what I know," I said.

"Hmmm," said Mr. Graham. "Well, you know your own mind. I like this one, Ellen," he continued, changing the subject completely, taking a long drag on his cigarette.

We were seated in the parlor of Mr. Graham's house.

Deshi slipped silently into the room. He placed a platter of fruit on the table with a deferential nod in my direction. Deshi was Mr. Graham's houseboy. He must have been only a few years older than me, and he treated me like a queen. Deshi had high cheekbones and delicate features. His sloe eyes widened and narrowed with feline intensity. He slid in and out of rooms like a moonbeam.

"I'm going to draw Deshi," I said.

"With or without clothes," Mr. Graham quipped. Then he caught himself. "Yes, of course you are," he laughed. "You are going to draw the world. Such a talent."

I felt my ears burn.

"But, regard your present assignment."

My assignment was the long-legged, narrow-hipped form of a naked woman poised on the verge of a high dive. Her nipples, rising from a pair of perfect globed breasts, followed the point of her chin. I'd used white highlights and ochre oil pastels to suggest sunlight on burnished flesh. I had loved drawing her. She was radiant.

"I don't know if I approve of the poetry, here," Mr. Graham observed, his green eyes gathering in a squint. "It's a little off-putting. And the crayons, the oil pastels, are terribly messy."

He rubbed his thumb and forefinger together as if trying to clean them. Then he rose from the desk. Mr. Graham wore a short cotton kimono over his dark-colored slacks. He had on socks and corduroy slippers.

"Have some fruit, Ellen," he said indicating the platter that Deshi had placed on the table. "I'm so glad you could come to lunch."

"Deshi," he said, addressing his white-coated houseboy. "Please bring sake and something for Ellen to drink."

Deshi vanished. As Mr. Graham had suggested, I addressed the platter of fruit. Deshi had arranged wood shavings around the fruit in a fine balsa nest. I grabbed a big peach nestled in the excelsior. The peach was juicy and sweet, an unexpected treat in the middle of winter.

"They're hothouse peaches," Mr. Graham explained. "They're from Kyoto. They're lovely when they get here, but Deshi brings them to perfection. He wraps each one in a tea towel. He broods over them like a hen over its eggs until they have ripened completely. Deshi never loses a peach."

Deshi had made a small cross at the top of each peach so the skin would peel off in four leaf-shaped swaths. Eating them must have been an art as well, one that I hadn't mastered. I wrestled with the slippery softball-sized fruit. The peach juice drizzled down my forearm.

"What's the right way to eat these?" I asked, my hands growing stickier with every bite.

"Simplicity's best," Mr. Graham responded cryptically. He dabbed my chin with a napkin. "In a few moments, we'll have the surprise," he added warmly, "but first I must have my sake."

Deshi entered on cue with a plain wooden tray. He poured hot rice wine from a rough pint-sized carafe into an equally rustic cup, then raised a second extravagantly painted porcelain bottle aloft.

"And some plum wine for you?" Mr. Graham inquired. I nodded. I was never allowed to drink wine at home. Deshi filled a cordial glass almost up to the brim with a thick amber liquid.

The plum wine was sweet and syrupy. It fell in a burning waterfall down through my body. I was suddenly warm and deliriously happy sitting in Mr. Graham's house with Deshi as my attentive handmaiden. At school, Mr. Graham was pretty discreet and controlled, but his preferential treatment embarrassed me.

"I prefer you when you aren't self-conscious," Mr. Graham observed, watching me over his cup.

Deshi brought more sake and Mr. Graham finished a second bottle.

"So, Ellen," he asked, draining the thimble-sized cup in a single gulp, "do you like my house?"

I was very impressed with Mr. Graham's house. It was lovely. Tatami-carpeted, simple—like the best Japanese homes. And it was full of wonderful things: books, cameras, microscopes, magazines, rocks. Deshi had arranged them all into small works of art. The resinous smell of pine and cedar perfumed the rooms.

"This house," Mr. Graham continued, "is a haven—a haven from girls and white gloves and the pressures of mothers to marry. It's a haven from business and expectations, from social engagements and parties and proving a great disappointment. Which I have. I always have."

Mr. Graham shook his head sorrowfully, poured and consumed one more small cup of sake.

"I inherited this house from a college friend," he continued. "He was living here in Japan. I inherited Deshi too. His name isn't even Deshi, really. That's what my friend named him. My friend was here on a fellowship. He was studying Japanese drama. I think "deshi" means dresser or something—an assistant in the Kabuki theater. So, it was a joke calling him Deshi. But a good joke, hmmmm?"

Mr. Graham was getting plastered. He leaned against a bookcase trying to smoke his cigarette, almost knocking over a silvery nautilus shell balanced on a delicate lucite stand, when Deshi entered with more sake.

"Thank you, Deshi," he said with a slight slur of the "s."

"Where was I? Oh, yes," he remembered, continuing his soliloquy.

"My friend went back to the States before long. He hated being alone. And I was his beneficiary. I got his house. Great friend . . . great friend."

"I'm thirty-three years old," Mr. Graham confessed suddenly with a sour laugh. "I'm thirty-three and I hide here. I am stranded in life. I hide here because I don't know what else to do." His voice rose and broke on a high note. He immediately tossed back another cup of warm sake.

Mr. Graham was drunk as a piper. I was a little high, too.

"Well," he said, "let's look at the surprise, now, shall we? Deshi, a little more wine."

I noticed the slightest hesitation on Deshi's part. He made one more trip to the cupboard. The surprise was a box wrapped in brown tissue paper. It was tied with a green raffia cord.

"I wrapped it," Mr. Graham proudly announced. "Deshi helped." He winked. "Open it," he commanded.

I tore through the wrapper.

Inside the box was a stack of old illustrations of the strangest birds I had ever seen. One was a pink flamingo with a big orange beak that looked like Jimmy Durante's nose. It's long neck was looped like a bow. Another was a small-eyed white ibis. It had a beak like needle-nosed pliers. A wood stork, its featherless head a grisly, iron-clad helmet, an elegant crested night heron, and a stout pelican, its pendulous pouch full of fish, were also among the pictures.

"It's a gift from me," Mr. Graham said leaning toward me. "Strange birds for a very strange girl." His hand came to rest on my knee and moved up to my thigh.

"Don't do that," I said lackadaisically.

The plum wine was working on me. I felt good, and his hand felt good, gently massaging its way up my thigh.

"All right, Ellen," he said. But his hand continued to move up my leg.

I've always wondered who invented the dress. Dresses remind me of lampshades. It's easy to get up inside them. Mr. Graham's hand reminded me of a moth fluttering in between a lampshade and a bulb.

"Don't do that," I repeated without much conviction.

Deshi stepped into the room with more sake. Noting that Mr. Graham had his hand up under my skirt, he reddened. He made a very deep bow. Mr. Graham drew back his hand.

"Of course you are right, Ellen," he said quickly. "You are only the artist. You are the artist aren't you?" His speech was ginny and muddled.

"Yes," I said, trying to look righteous. "I am the artist."

"Of course you are," he repeated. "No need to take umbrage. No need." He leaned closer to me and he began stroking my hair.

"Forgiven, I hope," he said.

I didn't reply. I was watching Deshi watch us.

"Of course I'm forgiven," he muttered, his hands still caressing my head. "Yes, you are the artist, my dear. You are the artist. We have time for a little more wine," he added, falling back onto the soft-pillowed couch. "One more glass of wine. Then, Deshi, call a cab. It's time for Ellen to leave." He half-swooned onto the cushions. Deshi moved swiftly to his side and propped him up on the sofa. Deshi reminded me of a puppet master in the bunraku puppet theater. Grandmother had taken me, once, to see the bunraku puppets in Tokyo. They were life-sized puppets that looked disturbingly human. The bunraku puppeteers manipulated them onstage in full view of the audience. The puppeteers were dressed all in black and the audience had to pretend not to see them moving the puppets around. As with anything where one pretends long enough, soon the puppeteers really did become almost invisible. They disappeared into the background. I saw only the puppets moving, as if by their own volition. Deshi rearranged Mr. Graham into a polite position on the couch. Mr. Graham now looked rather composed.

"Ellen," he said, "I'm so sorry to say good-bye to you this way, but Deshi will take care of you. Deshi, call Ellen a cab."

Deshi dipped slightly and fled from the room. He was mortified by Mr. Graham's sudden collapse. I heard his voice on the telephone requesting a cab.

"Good-bye, Deshi," I said later, at the door. Deshi nodded very politely, stepped out, paid the driver, and darted back

NAMAKO : SEA CUCUMBER 155

into the house quick as moonlight disappearing behind a drawn curtain.

Two weeks later, a dreadful thing happened.

"Ellen, I want to talk to you."

Gene stood in front of me holding my biology notebook. I already felt sick to my stomach. That morning I hadn't been able to find it. Later, in school, I'd asked Mr. Graham if he had given it back.

"Of course," he said carelessly, taking a drag from his cigarette. "You had two drawings for me this time, remember?"

"Yes, I remember," I said crossly, "but I thought you might have it. You see, it's missing. I can't find it."

"Well, hadn't you better?" he asked with an eyebrow raised. "It could prove very embarrassing."

"Yes. Yes, I have to find it. I must have just misplaced it."

And now here was Gene, my father, holding the very notebook, the one full of drawings of naked and near-naked women. They had replaced the crustaceans and mollusks that had once been my subjects of study. Those easily explained why phyla and their members had been replaced by my anatomical explorations of Homo sapiens, of the female gender.

"Ellen, I think this is yours," Gene said, indicating the red, spiral-bound notebook.

"Where did you get that?" I stammered. I could feel the blood rush to my face.

"It was on the sidewalk in front of the house."

It must have slipped out of my book bag.

"Is it yours?" he asked.

What could I do? Tell the truth? Certainly not.

"No, it's not mine," I lied, trying to remember if I'd been stupid enough to put my name in it. Gene saw right through me, of course. It wasn't enough to deny ownership. I had to produce a believable suspect.

"That notebook is Anne's," I blurted out. "Anne must have dropped it out on the sidewalk. Gee, I doubt if she knows it's missing."

"Really?" Gene asked rather coolly. "Whose drawings are in it?" I was sure he didn't believe me.

"Anne's drawings," I said. "It's her notebook. It must be full of her drawings."

"Well, if it's Anne's, I think she'll be sorry to discover it lost."

Gene must have been terribly disappointed in me. I wasn't even doing the honorable thing.

"I suggest you return it to her as soon as you can."

Gene handed the notebook back to me. I grabbed for it, but he didn't release it at once.

"I don't know what to think," he said softly, still hanging onto the notebook. "I didn't show this to Sara. I trust, Ellen, that you know what you're doing."

I took back the notebook.

"I'll tell Anne that you found it," I mumbled.

"Tell Anne that you found it," he said. "That way she won't be embarrassed."

"Yeah, thanks," I muttered and ran to my room, threw myself on the bed, and covered my head with a pillow.

I couldn't believe that Gene had looked through my notebook, a notebook full of the pictures I'd drawn for Mr. Graham. I thumbed quickly through it, just to torture myself. Yes, it was my notebook all right, raw and uncensored, with my signature style in every one of the drawings. I was sure that Gene knew that it wasn't Anne's, but he hadn't argued with me. He hadn't accused me. He just handed the notebook back. He was probably just as embarrassed as I was. Maybe I could pretend that I'd actually broken my hand several months before and hadn't been able to draw. Maybe I should break my hand to add an element of truth to the story. I concluded that this was a pretty ridiculous idea; one that indicated just how desperate I was. I couldn't look Gene in the eye after that, and tried to avoid him, though I noticed that he seemed to handle me with a great deal of care. He began to treat me with special attention. It was as if I had all of a sudden become some kind of person, someone that he could no longer ignore.

In the end, I gave the notebook to Mr. Graham and told him that he could keep it. I told him about Gene's finding it. I didn't tell him that I lied and said it was Anne's.

"Did you tell him about me?" Mr. Graham asked. "Does he know why you drew those pictures?"

"Of course not," I answered. "Do you think I wanted to get in more trouble?"

"Well, good. Very good," Mr. Graham said sagely. "Ellen, I think you're a very wise girl."

11

mirugai |
long neck clams

We were bouncing along the road in Mr. Nielson's dusty station wagon, driven by a short Japanese driver with bad breath and a crew cut. On the road in front of us, the license plate of Mr. Nielson's white Buick disappeared and reappeared through the dust, like a hypnotist's glove. I don't know why we always seemed to take back roads to Aomori. Maybe they only seemed like back roads. We were on our way to one of those shows at which Mr. Nielson's dogs won ribbons. My parents and Mr. Nielson's wife, Linda, were also in the white Buick. The children and dogs were packed into the station wagon.

The desolate countryside raced by, gray and lifeless. The dogs were slobbering onto the backseat where I sat with Samuel, Mimi, and Gray. Mimi slid around on the front seat like a marble on a well-waxed floor. I was relieved that I did not have to sit by the driver, preferring the hot doggy breath of the Akitas. The man seemed to find every pothole in the road. I wondered if his feet, on those short legs, really reached the car pedals, for he seemed to drive, elbows out from the wobbly steering wheel, legs swinging, like a gnat on an elephant. Samuel and Gray were fidgeting in their usual manner, sliding their baseball cards back and forth between them on the seat. They were leaning way over the front seat back, over Mimi's head, their hands reaching out toward the dash. The driver seemed to take no notice of this. He was preoccupied with the other car, and its license plate, bouncing along ahead of us. We were winding our way from Hachinohe to the real "northern country," and the weather was gray and cold. The roads in this area were often unfinished. Mr. Nielson loved to travel these side routes, his white car trouncing along like a bat out of hell.

We stopped at the beach. The dogs had to get out and walk to stay fresh for the show, otherwise they became cross and ill-tempered. The children too were allowed to run for a bit and for much the same reason. The desolate strip of sand before us seemed to stretch out like a desert. The sea had receded so far that the broken bits of shell that pebbled it were exposed. They made the beach seem sad and more like a graveyard. The wind whipped around us, mingling with the salt air, twisting our hair into ropes. Mrs. Nielson's colorful scarf and dark glasses distinguished her as a woman of mystery. She spoke to us only rarely, and then only with caution, as if we were unreliable creatures. She and Sara stood by the white Buick, not speaking, their eyes turned toward the sea. Mr. Nielson and Gene drank a couple of beers. Sara took a big basket out from the backseat of their car, and dipping her hands into it, pulled out sandwiches wrapped in wax paper. We did not need to be called. It was as though we had radar. We hovered about like flies. Mimi had peanut butter and jelly. Gray had bologna. Gene's sandwich was a particular one, ham and cheese with mustard, horseradish, tomato and pickle. Sara unwrapped each sandwich, looking for it, announcing the others as she came across them, her hands stretched our way each time in offering. Gene and Mr. Nielson settled into their sandwiches. Samuel, Mimi, and Gray squabbled and fussed like seagulls; Sara and Mrs. Nielson smoked, looking out toward the distant sea. The driver was still wrestling with the car, on tiptoe now, his shaved head lost somewhere under the hood, the sandwich Sara had given him perched precariously on the edge of the roof. The air smelled thickly of salt and fish. Something that looked like the body of a seal lay stretched a ways up the beach. Maybe it was driftwood. Then, the small figure of Mimi, alone in grayness and wind, made its way up the beach in an uncertain progress, stooping for shells, straightening, putting them into pockets, heading toward the faraway tide. Behind me, I heard the doors of the Buick slam and then Samuel and Gray's voices, sounding thin and desolate as sea birds, calling her name, the wind blowing it back in their faces.

"Mimeeee, Mimeeee."

Mimi heard it, and looked back at them, then, again, toward the sea, as though she were considering something. Then she picked her way tediously back toward us. The sand seemed to cling to her steps, as though the beach tried to hold onto her, giving her up only grudgingly.

The driver was already gathering the dogs into the car. I returned to the backseat, now gritty with all of the sand Samuel and Gray had trailed in. The white Buick, loaded with adults, waited ahead, hunched like a ghost, until we were all in our car. Bumping our way back onto the semblance of road, we resumed our journey.

We recognized our destination at once by all of the cars, the barking, and the din. A crowd milled around behind ropes. Loudspeakers played popular Japanese lyrics, punctuated by the machine-gun chatter of a Japanese announcer. We piled out in our usual tumble—dogs and kids—while the adults, craning their necks, sidled their way through the crowds. Mr. Nielson, a cigarette hanging out of his mouth, put his dogs on their big leashes and guided them around the crowd. The ground was damp and muddy. The air smelled like dog feces, urine, and fish. A Japanese man with knee-high rubber boots and a cap on his head greeted Mr. Nielson, admiring his dogs. Mr. Nielson's chest puffed out as he gestured toward Jiro, speaking softly and quickly in Japanese. Jiro was there merely because of his beauty. He was all white, instead of the proper Akita colors, so it was impossible for him to win a prize, but Mr. Nielson liked to show him off to the other Akita owners. His other two dogs had good chances to win.

Mimi and the boys ran back and forth to makeshift refreshment stands near the swamp of automobiles, wagons, and bicycles. Sara and Gene chatted with the mysterious Linda Nielson, whose long black hair was wound around and around on top of her head so that it looked like a pillbox hat. We rarely saw Mrs. Nielson. She was a mystery to us since she had no children and exhibited none of the motherly traits that we expected of women her age.

I hung back. A few teenage Japanese schoolboys in their black uniforms and caps eyed me inquisitively. I tried to blend into the crowd. I had lost Sara and Linda Nielson, who were now standing somewhere close to the ropes. One of the boys came up to me and said something to me in Japanese, expecting me to comprehend. I mumbled a stupid response.

"Ah," he said, his eyes wide, switching proudly to English, "You are American." His accent was thick.

"Yes," I said dumbly.

"We are from Sapporo," he said with the slightest bow and indicated his friends. I saw from the corner of my eye that they were all watching us expectantly, big smiles on their faces, ready to rush in my direction and make a big scene. I noticed Gene approaching from another direction, preoccupied, his eyes on the crowd, a scowl on his face and his cigarette dangling from one side of his mouth. His rumpled trousers hung beneath the still sharp creases of his heavily starched shirt.

"Excuse me," I said, hurriedly making my way toward him, away from the too-polite boy. I fussed up to Gene, grabbing his hand and smiling engagingly. "Daddy," I chirped falsely, "Let's go look at the dogs. Have you seen them?"

He looked at me strangely, taken off guard, trying to figure out just what I was up to. Gene was always a little suspicious of me. Then, smiling broadly, he said, "All right, Ellen. Come on. I guess we can find Sara later." I hooked my arm confidently in his and did not look back over my shoulder to see what went on with those boys.

The dog show, in my opinion, was intolerable. I walked around it with Gene for a while. He was making bets on the dogs that would win. He was in a great mood, laughing with the Japanese men, a notebook in one hand, a pen in the other. And the Japanese men were shaking their heads and handing over their yen, which Gene gave to me to hold. I guess I looked like the perfect banker—neutral and disinterested. Unfortunately, the dogs Gene was betting on did not perform as expected, so he had to make lots of paybacks. I didn't give back all the money he'd given me. I kept a wad of bills in my pocket. Gene came up short.

"Ellen," he asked, as I handed over the fistful of blue-and-red bills, "where is the rest of the money?"

"That's all there is," I lied.

Gene looked at the money. I could see grave disappointment written all over his face.

"Well," he said, "so that's all there is." Then he looked at me closely, raising an eyebrow. "Well, Ellen," he said, "it looks like for some reason I owed you something."

Then he put one hand on my shoulder and squeezed, digging deeper into his pockets to pay off his debts, and guiding me back through the crowd.

For the rest of the show, I hung around Sara, Gene, and the Nielsons, like a third wheel, asking ridiculous questions so they wouldn't ignore me. Mr. Nielson's dog, Tomodachi, took second prize; Babysan third. By the time the show was over, it had started to rain. The mud was deepening around us. The crowd made it worse. Mr. and Mrs. Nielson were socializing with Sara and Gene. The dogs, excited, strained upon their leashes. The Japanese schoolboys, offended, were pretending that I wasn't there. I was feeling guilty and incredibly out of place. Mimi, covered with mud where she'd slipped and fallen, was running around undeterred. Samuel and Gray were climbing under the ropes, petting dogs, laughing loudly, and clowning for the Japanese men. I saw the Japanese schoolboy watching me as I was loaded into the station wagon along with the children and all the dogs. He squared his shoulders and broke into a superior smile. I closed my hand around the yen in my pocket, the money I'd stolen from Gene. We seemed to sit for an eternity while the adults continued to converse, their hands on the car doors as though they were ready to depart. Then, suddenly, we were leaving, a dirty caravan embarking upon the long trip home.

The wet fur of the dogs smelled. Samuel and Gray were sluggish. Mimi, sprawled like a small crab on the front seat, was fast asleep. On the back of the driver's buzz-cut head, I could see tiny gray-yellow scars shining between the two faucet-shaped ears. He was humming some Japanese melody from the loudspeaker at the dog show over and over. I pressed my forehead against the window to cool it. My face felt damp and clammy, and my mouth, cottony. We

rocketed a zigzag course over the filthy switchbacks. The
car was full of the thickness of the afternoon, the dogs,
and everyone's breath. We crawled into a tiny village. The
muck-covered automobiles came to a heavy stop. Car doors
slammed and, again, Mimi, Samuel, and Gray rolled out,
rewound, inexhaustible. I sat in the steamy car for a while,
pressed against the sticky vinyl upholstery of the backseat,
until the driver opened the door on my side, gesticulating
and firing away at me in a language that no longer even
sounded like Japanese, but something coarse and ugly.
Getting out slowly, I pushed back my bangs; I was sweating.
They were plastered against my forehead. I waved him
away like an insect. Then I wandered off behind the others
along the rows of makeshift stalls of corrugated tin, old
tarps, and pungent straw. Samuel, Mimi, and Gray were
running back and forth, wrinkling their noses, and gasping at
the novel assortment of things, live and dead, being sold.
Sara and Linda Nielson were making deals with the vendors
who were laughing and nodding their kerchiefed heads and
wrapping up handfuls of things in wet newspapers. The
village women's round faces shone like polished shells. There
were a few colorful streamers fluttering here and there in
the gray breeze. All the fishstuffs seemed to have eyes. There
was a small boy with a deeply scarred face and a deformed
hand, selling goldfish that looked like orange flags, and black,
pop-eyed fish in plastic, water-filled bags. Slime, and more
slime, slithered across the soiled straw and in the green
brackish water in buckets. Tangles of black-green eel and

squid and a gagging fish stink mingled with the growing sourness of my stomach.

Then I saw them piled in a heap, in a wooden frame. They were a tumble of clam shells, dark and pitted, and from each one extended a protuberance, long and gum-colored, as thick as Mimi's small wrists and shaped like an elephant's trunk. As I stared, some contracted spastically. Others undulated, curled, and uncurled. I walked behind one of the stalls and threw up, heaving until my insides felt raw, my head pinched and strangling. I could no longer breathe. Feverish and weak, I used the yen in my pocket to wipe off my mouth and chin. The mud at my feet was littered with the dirty blue-and-red bills.

———

I was horribly ill. It turned out that my gut was infested with parasites, probably from eating at foodstalls at the fair. I imagined them nibbling away at my innards, raising families, building roads in soft intestinal tissue. I couldn't eat solid food. If I tried to, my belly swelled and distended. The doctor took specimens—blood, feces, urine. Sometimes I would see Dr. Kimura looming above me. *An oni, a devil,* I thought, *coming to finally take me away*.

"I remember you," I mumbled. "You were in the Daimyô. You followed me here. Go away. Go away. You're trying to kill me. You are killing my grandmother. Go away."

The nurse held a syringe aloft. The doctor jabbed it into my arm. I rolled around in bed in a fever. I lost weight. And all the time the doctor hovered over me. I looked like a starving child.

Grandmother gave up her room for me. She moved in with Mimi. I was the sick person now.

"The color seems to be coming back to your grandmother's cheeks," Sara said, trying to be cheerful. "I think rooming with Mimi agrees with her."

She sat on the edge of the bed. The back of her hand rested lightly upon my forehead. I was in near-isolation. Dr. Kimura thought I might be contagious. Sara was worried that I'd miss the last weeks of school.

"You, on the other hand, are burning up. Your poor little face is on fire," she said.

I felt my mouth shape the word, "water." Sara put a straw to my lips.

She looked so beautiful leaning over me. Her face filled my whole horizon. I wanted to tell her about that, about how her words came out of her mouth like luminous eggs and broke over my face, cooling it, but I couldn't speak. I was falling, sucked into a whirlpool that was turning and turning, carrying me away from her.

"Sara," I tried to cry. "Sara, come get me," but she was so far away that I couldn't reach her. I turned my face to the darkness.

I awoke at the base of a lightless shaft. A dark flight of stairs led downward. I followed them into a cavern. Passageways snaked off in every direction. I chose one, making shaky progress, feeling my way on the wet rock walls, and arrived in a gloomy chamber. I could hear the gurgle of water behind the stone walls. I was surprised to see Grandmother standing in the cave. She wore a white silk kimono. In front of her was a child in a high wooden chair. She was feeding it worms. She turned when I entered. Her mouth tightened, lips pursed.

"You have a small soul," she said.

I fled from the room into the winding galleries. There were doors in the stony walls. I kept trying to find one to lead me out of the maze. Every door that I opened had monsters behind it. I pushed one open only to find a hunchback with a human heart in his hands. I closed it quickly. Behind another were two ghouls with knives. They were laughing and cutting away one another's skin.

Grandmother found me and grabbed my hand. Hers was so warm. She seemed suddenly caring. I wasn't afraid of her. We started to run together.

"Hurry up, child," she said. "Hurry up."

Up ahead was a ladder that led up into a circle of light. We were running toward it. But Grandmother was melting. She was turning into water. Her white kimono puddled onto the floor. I found I was holding only her hand. Her clothing had formed a pool at my feet. In the pool's center was part of a face—two eyes and a mouth floated mournfully on the surface.

"Go," the mouth said. "Go quickly, before it's too late."

There was warning in the eyes.

I let go of the hand and ran for the ladder. It turned into slippery fluid as I touched it. I couldn't climb it. I kept sliding down. I tried, but I slipped back again and again. I was crying, sobbing, and choking. The ladder kept sloughing off fluid. I couldn't scale it. I was soaking wet, from the ladder and my tears.

This time when I awoke I was back in my bed. It was comfortingly solid. I had peed in it. My fever had broken.

It was strange how quickly they moved me back in with Mimi. The doctor pronounced me completely recovered. According to Sara, he'd saved my life. I could hear the reproach in her voice when she said this. She seemed to be pointing out that my opinion of him had been unfair. As for Dr. Kimura, I noted that he looked thinner and older than he'd looked before. When I thanked him, as Sara had instructed, he seemed to lose all his composure.

"I did my best," he said humbly, eyelids lowered, "but, I failed." Dr. Kimura's face seemed to have caved in, giving it a skeletal quality. "I could do nothing, though I tried," he said. "You should not be alive. I am not the one who saved you."

Ineko-san sanitized Grandmother's room. I found out later that Grandmother's health had taken a nosedive. Mimi was glad that I was back in the room.

"Obachama's scary," she said.

"What do you mean, Mimi?" I asked. Mimi wasn't one to make judgments like that.

"Well, Ellen, at first it was fine, and I liked her being here. But then she started to burn incense and say creepy prayers. And she went to your room every night and sat in the chair, just staring at you. Then she got sicker, and now she looks like an obake. She's scary, and I'm glad she's not in here with me anymore."

"So, I guess that means you're happy I'm here."

"Oh, yes, Ellen," Mimi purred. "I'm so glad you're back."

12

usagi |
rabbit

Mimi's threats of running away had finally erupted into action. She stood in the genkan doorway, cradling a torn paper sack stuffed with her clothes and announced her departure. The deciding factor—she had been required to wear a pleated skirt to her first grade class. The hairband had gone on easily enough, so had the white blouse and the embroidered sweater, but the skirt had incited a battle. Exhausting the efforts of Sara and Ineko-san, Mimi emerged from her room in the morning with her hairband askew and her white blouse untucked and already rumpled. She had on a pair of orange knee socks that clashed mightily with the red of her sweater. Her scabby brown knees glared from beneath the sharp pleats of the skirt. Samuel and Gray nudged one another and laughed arrogantly. Mimi, skirted, left for school in humiliation.

Sara put Mimi on a public bus. That's how we all got to school. Mimi was having a very bad day. She missed her stop, and the bus driver couldn't take her back until he had finished his run, so she was an hour late that morning. Later in the day, she was kicking rocks on the playground and her shoe flew off her foot and hit another kid in the forehead. Finally, she repeated one of the songs that she had learned from David Vintner and was sent home in disgrace. Sara scolded her for her contrariness, and sent her to her room "to think about it." That period of seclusion had resulted in the bagful of clothes. Mimi wore the same blouse, sweater, and hairband, but the skirt had been replaced with a pair of old corduroy pants. She announced, glumly, that she was running away and that she was never coming back.

Ineko-san made a big fuss, retrieved an empty overnight case and handed it to Mimi sighing, "Ineko-san, 'bye, bye.'"

Sara said, "Mimi, this is not really what I had in mind when I told you to think about it. Are you certain it's the right thing to do?"

Samuel and Gray watched Mimi closely to see what she would do. Mimi glared at them. They were the real source of her fury.

Two days before, Samuel had been awarded the honor of being able to walk Mr. Nielson's dogs. He'd enlisted Gray's aid. Mimi had begged Samuel to let her help, too, but he had refused.

"No, Mimi." Samuel had said. "These dogs are big dogs. You're too little."

It was the ultimate insult.

"Gray's only a year older than me." Mimi argued. Samuel held firm. Mimi felt discriminated against just because she was a girl. The skirt situation was salt on an already large wound.

Mimi was surprised by Sara and Ineko-san's easy acceptance of her decision to run off. In answer to Sara's question she nodded sullenly. The point was now one of honor. She dropped into the genkan where her favorite shoes waited like a couple of tired soldiers. She slipped them on and pushed open the heavy front door. When she turned, her short, jet-black hair fanned out like a little umbrella around her head.

"Mimi-chan, bye, bye. Sayonara," Ineko-san called sadly, her sorrow belied by the smile on her lips.

The bag clutched to her chest, Mimi made her way out of the gate and up the gravel driveway.

"Sara, do you want us to follow her?" Samuel and Gray volunteered.

"No," Sara answered harshly. Samuel and Gray exchanged worried glances.

While the boys were busy discussing Mimi's exile, an object lesson in self-direction, Sara beckoned to me. She frowned.

"Ellen," she said. "You'll keep an eye on her, won't you?"

I was relieved by Sara's concern. I had faced, for a moment along with Samuel and Gray, the specter of her disregard. "Sure," I said merrily. Spying agreed with me. I enjoyed it. Sneaking from the house, I followed Mimi, tagging her slow, sullen steps to the dirt road and across the farm fields toward the Japanese machi. She took the rough path that cut through the sunflowers. The sunflowers looked down on her. The tall, green stalks rustled softly. In the distance, at the farmer's compound, a motor of some sort whined on endlessly in the slow, autumn stillness. Mimi's progress was slow. Her bag full of clothes was too full to carry. It was tearing. Pieces of clothing kept falling out onto the road. Finally, she threw down the bag and plunked down beside it. She sat dejectedly on the roadside margin of dirt and weeds looking downcast, a forlorn figure in the distance from my vantage point on the road far behind her. I was almost at the point of striding toward her to guide her back, when she got up sluggishly. She kicked the bag around, knocking her clothes all over the place. Then she picked up her bag and wobbled back up the road toward home, but she kept dropping clothes, so she made slow progress. It was easy to get home before her.

I slipped into the house and kept watch from a window. Mimi crept stealthily into the yard. She snuck up to her rabbit, grabbed it from the hutch, and huddled under the very window from which I was peering. Then, cuddling it tightly, Mimi poured her misery out to her rabbit, sniveling into its fur. I reported the whole thing to Sara who was not very surprised.

"Samuel, Gray," she said strictly, "stay in the house."

She summoned Ineko-san. Sara and Ineko-san stood together not far from the window under which Mimi crouched in despair. Then the two women put on an outstanding performance.

"Oh, what shall I do?" Sara cried to the maid. "My poor little Mimi is gone."

"Mimi-chan, kawai so ni, ne," Ineko-san agreed pitifully.

"Yes," Sara continued, "The poor baby. But, I am the sad one. Oh, how I wish she hadn't left me. I think she has broken my heart."

Ineko-san put her arm around Sara, and they both wept. We heard a rustle under the window. I peeked over the windowsill into the garden. Mimi was pressing her bunny back into its cage. Then she was at the genkan doorway, her eyes bleary with tears. She rushed, unseeing, past Ineko-san, past all of us, and fell into Sara's arms, where she cried until we thought she could not cry anymore, and, finally exhausted, fell asleep. Sara carried Mimi to the bedroom and tucked her carefully between the crisp, white sheets of the narrow twin bed.

It turned out that the boys' new job was a bone of contention. Mimi was not the only one it upset. Samuel wouldn't let Gray walk all the dogs. He let him walk Baby-san, and some of the other females, but Tomodachi and Jiro, the two powerful males, he considered his personal charges. Gray, of course, wanted a turn at each one.

"No, you're too little," Samuel told him in the same tone he'd used on Mimi.

Bad-tempered Gray was furious, but Samuel wouldn't relent. He took his new duties seriously, proud that he was able to use the velvet leashes and collars to keep the big dogs in check. Unlike Gray, he did not need to resort to a choke-chain. Samuel looked silly and pompous walking the bulky Akitas on their showy leashes. Gray was too small to walk those dogs, but so, for that matter, was Samuel.

"I get a dollar every time I take them out," Samuel bragged. Astride his bike in the circle of boys and girls, Samuel was basking in the green light of their envy.

"It's 'cause your Dad's big buddies with Mr. Nielson," Ryan Brynford said.

"It is not," Gray fired back in Samuel's defense. He might disagree with Samuel, but he was faultlessly loyal.

"Is so," Ryan shot back at him.

This is how Gray and Ryan got into their fights.

"Gaw, the man must be rich," Laird Brynford said nastily.

Just beyond the edge of the circle of children, Laird lounged, looking boneless, his arms draped over the handle-bars of one of his skeleton bikes. He wore the perpetual sneer that his buckteeth produced.

"How often do you walk 'em?" he demanded.

"Every day," Samuel responded. I could tell by the look in Laird's mean, blue eyes that he was doing a little arithmetic and probably over-taxing his brain.

"Jiro's the best dog," Samuel added with pride. The big white dog was his favorite. "He really responds."

"Well, I guess you hafta walk 'em every day, don't you?" Laird jeered. "They're prisoners, aren't they? Guess that sickening little swish they take with you is the only freedom they're ever gonna see." Yukking it up, Laird turned his bike toward the road. "You're no pal to those dogs. You're just another one of their jailers."

Samuel recoiled as if someone had slapped him. I think it was Laird's jealous remarks that caused all the trouble. If it weren't for Laird, none of the terrible things would have happened. If it weren't for Laird, Samuel wouldn't have let Jiro off his leash the next day, against Mr. Nielson's specific instructions. If it weren't for Laird, nothing would have happened to Mimi's rabbit, and most of all, Soft, our dog, wouldn't have died.

Because of Laird's taunts, Samuel disobeyed Mr. Nielson's orders. He let Jiro off his leash to run free. And Jiro didn't hesitate for even a second. He ran away over the farm fields toward the distant line of forest and Samuel couldn't retrieve him though he called and called, thus proving Sara's and Grandmother's assertion that "those dogs could go wild."

Samuel didn't come home. He was too ashamed. Gene had to hunt for him, asking the neighbors if they'd seen him. He drove from house to house in the Edsel with Gray and Mimi sitting in back. The Brynfords told Gene that they'd seen Samuel out in the farm fields with Jiro. Mr. Nielson complained irritably that Samuel had not come back with his dog. Armed with this information, Gene deposited Mimi and Gray at home and headed out over the fields.

It was dark. Silvery feathers of cloud, backlit by the moon, streaked the night sky. The sunflowers, drooping past their prime, looked like crowds of old men stooped in the shadows.

Gene took the dirt path, striking into them. He disappeared in their midst. Their legions seemed to close like a wall behind him. He found Samuel, silent with terror. It was bad enough that Gene had to hunt for him. Worse than that, though, was that he had to face Mr. Nielson. When Gene brought him home, Samuel's teeth were chattering, probably not just from the cold.

"What happened, Sam?" I asked.

He opened his mouth, but could not speak.

"Ellen," he finally croaked, his face white with terror. "I lost him, I lost Jiro. I lost Mr. Nielson's dog."

I imagined Jiro, the white Akita, out in the moonlit forest, his big pink tongue lolling between his teeth, gold eyes alight and wild. I imagined moles, bats, hopping hares, skunks. I imagined a lightning fast chase and fights with badgers and silver raccoons, the white dog spotted with blood, the savagery racing back into him. I stated the obvious.

"You're in really big trouble." I said.

"I know," Samuel said, his face twisted in misery. Every muscle in his body seemed tense.

"I don't know what to do, Ellen," he confessed. "I wish I could undo it. Mr. Nielson's going to kill me."

"Maybe not," I replied. "We'll go looking tomorrow. Maybe we'll find Jiro and everything will be okay." I tried to offer some comfort, but I did not believe it for a moment. And, of course, that is not what happened. Samuel's act had the worst possible outcome.

The bloody deeds must have taken place sometime during the first hint of day.

Still fuzzy from sleep, Mimi was the one who found what was left of her rabbit. She'd gone out to the yard to feed it, with the usual portion of oats and old lettuce leaves.

Maybe the moon had not even withdrawn, still dappling dawn with its light. Maybe the birds still slept soundly, as we did, and the world was still wrapped in silence. Maybe the wind rose and fell, alone, driving predators' smells before them, and the rabbit raised its head and chewed faster, its pink nose twitching frantically in its fringe of white whiskers. I can only think that its mind turned off, or that long before its torture, it had already died of fright. I don't know. I know when I fall and hurt myself badly, I don't feel anything. Something comes up like a wall between me and the pain. I hope this is what happened to Mimi's rabbit when it was maimed and destroyed. I tried to explain this to Mimi. She could not comprehend it. All she saw was the blood all over the rabbit's cage, the gore spread out over the grass and the two soft white pieces of ear.

The cage was turned over. There had clearly been a struggle. Entrails were strewn all over the yard. Mimi let out a long, slow wail. We ran from the house in our nightclothes. Mimi was squatting next to the tumbled-down hutch and the bits of flesh and fur. She was howling. We stood there in shock—Sara, Gene, Samuel, Gray, and I. It took us awhile to understand what we were seeing. There was blood and gore everywhere. There was Mimi crying and crying. Sara was the first to take action. She rushed to Mimi and wrapped her arms around her. Mimi's cries turned into muffled sobbing. It wasn't until Mimi quieted down that we heard another horrible sound. It was a whimper. Gray recognized it at once. It was Soft. Like beads strung together, our heads turned to the source of the sound. We all saw him at once, a small heap of blood and fur in the yard's far corner.

Gray covered the distance before the rest of us had registered what we had seen.

"No, oh, nooo," he wailed. "Soft, Soft. Oh, God. Dad, help him. Help him. He's dying. Dad, help him," he yelled.

We were frozen. Gene was at Gray's side within seconds, his hands on his shoulders. Gray's face was savage.

"Jiro," he spat. "It was Jiro. It's all Sam's fault. Sam, why did you let Jiro go? Look. Look, he killed Soft."

"Get inside. Sara, get them all inside." Gene didn't want us to see anymore, but it was too late. We all had seen Soft—what was left of him. He was badly mauled. Broken bones stuck out of his body. He was alive, but just barely. He shouldn't have been. He must have fought hard. It must have been terribly violent. Why hadn't we heard anything?

"It was Jiro," Gray said in the cold hell of his fury.

"No," Samuel yelled. "No, Jiro wouldn't do that." He was crying, too. Mimi's face was an "o" of horror. Sara herded her children into the house. Gene followed, pushing past us, moving with purpose. He went into his bedroom and came out with his shotgun. It was against the law to have a gun in Japan, but Gene kept one anyway, hidden away in his room. His friends had them too. Gene was a hunter. When we were in the United States, he used to bring deer home tied to the front of the car, hat pushed back, wearing a smile. This was different. There was no joy in his face, no loose smell of yellowing beer. There was anger and edge. He grabbed the gun and walked outside. We heard one shot. It was an explosion. It rocked through each of us, hit each of our hearts. Four dead little Indians. Then there was silence. We were glad when we heard the gunshot. We knew Soft was finally dead. Something we couldn't possibly fix had been ended. A horror removed, to be tucked forever away.

Only Gray was not ready to tuck it away. "You did it, Samuel," he accused. "You let Jiro go and you caused this."

"How d'you know it was Jiro, Gray?" Samuel shouted desperately. "How do you know?" "I know," said Gray. "Samuel, why did you let him go?" Gray was crying again when Gene walked tiredly into the house, his gun under his arm.

"Gray, go to your room," Gene ordered. "Samuel you come with me. We're going to find Nielson. We've got to put that dog down."

Samuel was white as a ghost. Mimi looked like she'd seen one.

"Go get your coat," Gene said.

Samuel did as Gene told him. He seemed suddenly very mature. He walked like a man at Gene's side, a condemned man going to face his death. They got into the car and drove off. Sara and Ineko-san cleaned up the yard. Mimi was sniffling. Gene had wrapped Soft in a sheet. The shroud lay in the corner of the yard. A big red stain had spread at the bottom. We never got to see Soft again, just a bloody winding sheet in the corner of the yard. There was nothing left of the rabbit.

News traveled fast. David Vintner came by on his tenspeed bike. I was out in the yard.

"What happened?" he asked.

"Soft is dead," I said miserably. And looking at Mimi, I added, "And Mimi's rabbit is dead." David looked as if lightning had hit him. I could almost smell the fire and the smoke.

"Mimi's rabbit," he repeated. "That bastard. Where's Sam?"

"Gene took him to Nielson's. Sam let Jiro go. Jiro did this. They're going for Jiro. They're going to put that dog down."

"No," David said. "No, they're wrong. Jiro didn't do it. I know who did it. Look, Ellen," he said, "get Gray. Go find Samuel. Don't let them kill Nielson's dog. I'll explain later." Then, he was off like a flash.

I didn't do what David told me. I paced with Mimi back and forth in the yard. Gray walked around muttering to himself. He'd walk over to Soft's little mummy and started crying all over again. Sara fretted over us, white-knuckled, especially worried about Samuel, who was out of her sight. Grandmother drifted out into the yard where we had gathered like prisoners of war or shell-shock sufferers. She walked over to Soft's body and stood, gazing sadly down on it.

"Fuzen no tomoshibi. Life is short," she said.

Then she walked to the white picket fence where it butted up against the sunflower field, and ran her hands through her hair. She had recently cut it short. She shook her head in a horsey way, as if she were trying to shake off a tether. She looked skinny and forlorn standing by the rickety fence. She looked like the abandoned tetherball pole.

Claire Vintner came running down the drive in her little red boots. She ran to Gray and grabbed his hand. "Quick," she said. "Gray, quick, you have to come quick. David's got him. He's fighting him. He's got Laird."

"What are you talking about?" Sara interrupted. It was really too much. It was madness. The children hysterical. Adults in shock. Dead animals. Fights. We had all become horrible savages.

"Oh," Claire said when she saw Sara. Her big, blue eyes went completely vacant. She was in awe of our mother.

"Claire," Sara said, "Claire, what are you talking about?"

Claire took a deep breath and tried to deliver her news. "David," she said. "David's fighting with Laird. He has bloody boots."

"Who?"

"Laird."

"He has two bloody rabbit's feet."

"Who?"

"Laird. So, David said, 'Laird, you killed that rabbit, didn't you,' and Laird said, 'Man, what do you care? It's not your rabbit.' And David said, 'You killed the dog, too, you bastard.' And Laird said, 'It was a weaselly mongrel. It deserved to die.' Oh, you better come, because David is killing him."

Sara said, "Children stay here." But she couldn't stop anyone. We were all right behind her. We jumped into the car, and she couldn't stop us. She didn't have time. Sara took the bumpy roads like a stunt driver. Claire sat up front and showed her the way.

David and Laird were fighting in the sunflower field, not far from the house. It was not far, actually, from the site of

David and Claire's infamous sideshow. When we got there, David had Laird in a headlock.

"Tell 'em," David said brutally. "Tell' em who killed their rabbit. Look at this," he said, quickly holding up a bloody white foot. " Tell 'em who killed their dog." Laird's eye was so swollen he couldn't see out of it. One whole side of his face was mashed and bruised. David's chin was cut and bleeding. Blood trickled out of his mouth. The flesh had been opened on his brow, over his eye.

"You fucker," Laird hissed at David. "Yeah," Laird snarled, glaring at us from under the crook of David's arm. "Yeah, I killed your rabbit, and I killed your damn dog. I wanted a lucky rabbit's foot, see. And I got one. In fact, I got two."

We stood there in horror. We stared at Laird Brynford, in shock.

Sara spoke. "David, let Laird go," she said sternly.

David looked surprised. He released Laird Brynford and Sara walked up to that murderer, so that she could look right at him, straight into his eyes.

"You killed a rabbit, Laird Brynford," she said. "You killed a dumb animal. You did it in darkness, and I'm not surprised. Because, Laird, you're a dumb animal too. You're just like that rabbit and that dog and, at some level, you know that. And you know that when your father hears about this, he's going to do something as bad to you as what you've done to that dog and that rabbit. And I'm sorry for that, Laird. I'm sorry because it's made you what you are. I'm sorry because it's going to hurt. And, I'm sorry to say, that all the rabbits' feet in the world aren't going to protect you. I think you know that, too."

Laird cringed at the mention of his father.

"Don't tell him," he whispered. It sounded like a prayer. "You won't tell him," he pleaded, spitting through his buckteeth, his voice shaking.

"Laird," Sara said, "I'm not going to say a word. I don't have to. In fact, there is no way anyone can stop him from hearing about it. He probably knows already."

We all heard the truth in Sara's words. Those words pushed the anger out of us, and they took out the fear. Laird looked pathetic. If we felt anything now, it was pity.

"Come on, children," Sara said quickly. "We have to stop this insanity. David, you come, too."

David looked over at Laird and followed, head bowed. His blows had been feeble compared to the one Sara'd dealt Laird. I knew that what Sara had done was, in some ways, worse than anything Markham Brynford would do. Sara'd shown him the truth. She'd shown Laird his pain, his anger, and his fear, and it was a horrifying thing. I saw Sara's hand come to rest on David Vintner's shoulder as we got into the car.

"David, thank you," she said. David turned bright pink. He nodded, embarrassed, and climbed into the station wagon.

I sat in front with Mimi and Sara. Claire, David, and Gray were in back. Sara shocked us again with her daredevil driving. We bounced and lunged over potholes that lifted us from our seats and slapped us back down as though we were attached to them with elastic.

We screeched to a stop in Mr. Nielson's driveway and tumbled from the car. There was no one in sight, but Gene's Edsel was parked in front of the house. Inside the compound, Mr. Nielson's Winchester rifle leaned against the chicken-wire fence. Mr. Nielson was a marksman. Gene said he killed things the way he drank whiskey—neat. The rifle was taller than Gray. Gray went crazy when he saw the gun.

"Oh, no," he cried. "They've done it. They've killed Jiro." He drawled out the "o" in Jiro so that it sounded just like a howl. This provoked a funeral wail in the kennels. Several dogs and pups emerged and watched us, tongues lolling. Jiro wasn't among them.

"Gray, your hysteria is starting to get on my nerves," Sara said.

The ruckus brought Mr. Nielson running. That was an unusual sight. Mr. Neilson was a big man. He was not of a size that we would have connected with speed.

"What the hell?" he said, stopping when he saw us gathered outside the compound. Gray flew at him. He threw his arms around Mr. Nielson's waist.

"I'm sorry," he screamed into Mr. Nielson's groin. Jiro didn't kill Soft. He didn't." Gray was choking. He was crying all over Mr. Nielson's pants. Mr. Nielson pried Gray's arms loose. By this time, Gene and Sam had also arrived at the kennel. Gray flew to them, clutching at each one.

"Dad," he said, grabbing a fistful of Gene's khaki slacks. "Sam," he moaned turning to Sam. "I was wrong. Wrong. Jiro didn't do it. Laird did it. Laird killed Soft. Jiro was innocent.

It's my fault." he said. "I thought Jiro did it, and now he's dead too."

"Gray," Sam said, hugging him gently. "Gray, Jiro is not dead. We found him. He's still alive. He's not going to die. You're right. They were going to shoot him. That was my fault. I let him go in the first place. But you just saved Jiro, Gray, you saved him. Do you hear me? That dog owes you his life."

This was more than Gray could stand. He'd been through too much. He collapsed onto Samuel with several chest-racking sobs. Gene came to Sam's aid, and the two of them led Gray to the Edsel.

Mr. Nielson said, "Damn near shot my dog for no good reason. Sara, you want a drink? I do."

Sara scanned our feverish faces. Escape must have seemed the sweetest of offers.

"Yes," she answered carelessly. "Yes, I could definitely use a drink."

"You kids can get cokes from the cooler out back," Mr. Nielson shouted over his shoulder. "But put the bottles back where you got 'em. I don't want that glass around the dogs."

We buried Soft that evening. Ineko-san stayed for the funeral. Gene dug a hole in the sunflower field, on the other side of the fence. Twilight kissed the backs of the sunflowers' heads. They were drooping under the weight of their burden of ripening seeds. Their huge faces were scarred from the attacks of insects and crows. Sara said Soft's shroud was too plain. She bundled his body in an old sheet covered with yellow flowers that had faded from too many washings. Gene let each of us throw a shovel of dirt on top of Soft. We all got to say a few words over the grave.

"Dust to dust," Gene said sadly.

"Soft, I love you," Sam whispered huskily.

"Soft, you're the bravest dog in the whole world. There will never be another dog like you." Gray said.

Mimi blew a kiss.

Sara said, "Soft was well-loved by all of my children. He was a fortunate dog."

Ineko-san offered, "Soft-san, sayonara. Bye, bye."

I said, "Soft's death was a crime, but it taught us to look for the truth."

Grandmother said nothing. She had already made her comments over the corpse.

I saw very little of David and Claire after that, although Sara asked after them often. It was known that David's mother was carrying on with an airman, that David's father had returned and found them together, that the two men had fought, and that David's father had left—this time, everyone thought, for good. Sara shared all this with us. David also went to the American school, but he was a year behind Anne and me because his grades were so bad, and he was a discipline problem. Sometimes he'd spend the whole day out in the halls, barred from his classes. He'd walk over to the air base—it was less than a mile from the school—and loiter around the hangers and watch the maintenance crews take apart planes.

The truth was, like Sara, I liked David Vintner. I liked everything about him. He'd earned my respect when he clobbered

Laird Brynford, but I kept my distance. In fact, the only occasions upon which we'd speak were our long waits at the bus stop. We took the same bus to the American school. We said very little. He'd ask about Sara. He seemed to be somewhat obsessed with her.

"Your mother is pretty amazing," he'd say.

"What do you mean?" I asked.

"Well, you can trust her, you know. Like, she'll always come through."

I guess it could have been true, though we'd never really tested Sara against that kind of expectation. I had a feeling she might not pass such a test. Sara was rather erratic. David had seen her at her best. I didn't have the heart to tell him that she wasn't always a star.

"Possibly," I replied, trying to be noncommittal.

It was early December. The snow was falling in great clumps around us. The bus was late, and the bus shelter was pathetically cold. We were all but marooned. It occurred to me that this was the essence of a David Vintner fantasy. I'd have to tell Anne. David told me he hadn't seen Sam lately. I replied that Samuel had a cold. Then David proceeded to entertain me with one of the lyrics for which he was highly acclaimed.

"Hey, Ellen, listen to this," he said. "It was a dark night, a scream was heard," he began. "For a man was hit by a flying turd."

He chanted line after memorable line, forcing the piece to its inevitable conclusion, "He could not scream. He could not float. And all the turds went down his throat," and stopped imperatively, pleased with himself. Of course, I had heard poems like it before from Samuel and Gray, but somehow I felt that David's delivery was invested with a particular grandeur and eloquence.

"That's thoroughly disgusting," I said.

The right response. He smiled. The snow swirled around us, enfolding our world in white. I felt like one of the delicate figures of a pair propped in the butter cream center on the top of a wedding cake. I could marry David Vintner, I thought. I could marry him and have his children.

David was laughing and talking about his airplane models, his hands mimicking their air patterns. He wasn't wearing gloves.

"Aren't your hands cold?" I asked quizzically.

David ignored me.

"I have a B-52," he said. "I don't even know if I want to paint it. It's a great color green."

His hands were really red and raw looking. He could get frostbite.

"Where are your gloves?" I demanded.

David stopped and looked at me, his eyes locked on mine. Then he looked down at his hands.

"What are you talking about?" he asked, his head cocked to one side, looking like his neck was broken.

"Your hands," I almost screamed. Now we were both looking at them. "Aren't they nearly frozen? Don't you have any gloves?"

It was strange to me, my voice. It had a screechy sound to it.

LINDA WATANABE McFERRIN   *190*

"I . . . don't have any," he confessed. "I don't have any gloves." His eyes had become cynical and hard.

"What?" I was shocked. "You don't have any gloves?"

David looked odd. His thin face seemed suddenly thinner.

"That's right," he said bitterly. "I don't have any gloves. You wouldn't understand what it is like. You have Sara. My mother's not like her. My mother. She doesn't know how to take care of anything. No wonder he left her. Anybody would leave her. She's so damned stupid. She buys me three leather jackets, and I don't even have one goddamn pair of gloves."

Then, incredibly, he was crying, his nose running, the tears streaming, wet, down his cheeks, streaking his face.

I sat, unbelieving, staring at him as he sobbed, afraid to touch him, afraid to open my mouth. The snow was piling in drifts around the shelter. There was no other sound than us. He took his hands from his face, which he had hidden in them and wiped them off on his jeans. Now he had only a runny nose and an occasional sniffle. He was under control again, but we no longer spoke. We sat there, in silence, just waiting for the bus to arrive.

13

yuki |
snow

It had been snowing for weeks. We'd known it was coming. There was always something different, a certain smell, a precise quality to the look and feel of the air that would tell us a storm was on its way. Grandmother was bundled up in aqua and clay-colored sweaters. The large wood stove near the kitchen was stoked every morning against the chill until it glowed like a red coal. We were warned not to touch it. The mountains of harvested sunflower stalks were blanketed in snow. We hadn't seen the plowhorse in weeks. Ineko-san had pulled the heavy silk futons down out of the closets to be used as quilts, and we lay at night crushed beneath them, like little bugs, flattened and pinned. Jars of canned foods from the store began filling the cupboards. Sara took us to the big machi and bought us two ski sweaters apiece. We saw less and less of the other children outside of school. They now stayed closer to home. One morning, Ineko-san showed us how the wet wash she'd hung out on the line had stiffened like boards in the cold. She brought in a piece, giggling, and Samuel,

Mimi, and Gray swarmed about it, amazed, fighting over who got to fold it. Gene seemed to drive here and there on a string of endless errands, while we grew impatient from all the winter preparation, almost holding our breath, our eyes on the windows or searching the rumbling gray sky, our heads resting at night on our pillows with one ear to the down and the other pricked to the unearthly-soft sound of falling snow. Then winter slammed down on us like a big, hard hand, and the world was draped, like a patient, in white. Ineko-san no longer came to the house every day.

Sara dragged out the books and games for when we were forced by weather to stay home from school and for when we were cramped up indoors, or we'd waddle around in the snowy drifts webbing the yard and the wide fields until we were tired of snow angels and igloos. The white continued to climb until only the snowplows could get through. We were thoroughly tired of it, taking it for granted as one might a flower garden or a beautiful mother.

I felt I had read all I could, having gone through five volumes of the World's Greatest Short Stories and enough Alfred Hitchcock magazines to skew me forever with a queer point of view. I was thick and crabby from being couped up in the house, but what I really missed, I concluded, was Anne. Most of the roads around had been plowed, and there seemed to be a break in the nearly relentless fall of the snowflakes.

I telephoned Anne. She'd received a new set of skis, and she wanted desperately to show them to someone. She didn't know how to use them yet. Sara told us that we would each be getting a pair of skis, even Mimi, so I decided that it would be a good idea to take a long look at Anne's and make some decisions about what to expect. Anne volunteered to come over. Mr. Matsuda offered to drive her in his new Land Rover with four-wheel-drive. I hung up the cream-colored phone, relieved. Samuel was staying over at a friend's house for the week, and Mimi and Gray were driving me crazy. Anne was not fond of my brother and sister. Part of her dislike for them dated back to an earlier visit when the two of them formed a horrible alliance and chased her from our house calling her names like "bug head" and teasing her as was their tendency with anyone who did not immediately smash them. It was not that Anne treated them poorly as a result. She treated them gingerly, as one might a pickle or some kind of sour fruit. I punished them for their rude manners. Now, they gave Anne a wide berth. So I was a little surprised when, after we'd thoroughly examined her skis and were prostrated upon the twin beds in my room drinking cokes and devouring a box of cookies, that Anne suggested we do something that included the two kids.

Ineko-san's clothesline, coiled out in back of the house, had caught her eye. She suggested we climb the white peaks that had formed in the fields around the house with the clothesline tied around our waists. I liked the idea and jumped at it. Anne and I were enamored with mountain climbing and climbers. Mimi and Gray were the perfect little novices to round out our party. They'd be dependent upon the outdoor expertise and guidance of experienced climbers like us. Mimi was wary. Gray was oblivious. He just wanted to get outside. They were not allowed to play out in the snow, when it was deep, by themselves.

Anne and I put some supplies into a knapsack and made Gray and Mimi carry it. They were docile as donkeys as we tied the clothesline around their waists and started out in our parkas and machi boots over the slick, newly-plowed roads. It wasn't long before we left the road entirely, cutting across the white fields. The going was tough, especially for the two little kids. A snow-covered hill loomed before us. We headed toward it. We did not think to question how these gigantic mounds had seemed to rise out of nowhere after the first snowfall. Mimi and Gray sank into the shimmering drifts, the snow creeping into the tops of their boots, but Anne and I were unconcerned. She was the first one up the hill. I brought up the rear, with Mimi and Gray tied in between us. They stumbled often, trudging uphill through snow that was up to their waists. Anne and I were patient. We pulled them out. We shouted encouragement. But their spirits started to wane. They grew cranky. They did not trust either of us. We were heartened when we crested the hill. Anne and I took out our flag. We'd taken one of Ineko-san's handkerchiefs and packed it in the knapsack. Now we tied it to Anne's walking stick, which was really a garden stake used to tie gladiolas. We thrust our flag into the snow. We had to push it in a long way for it to take hold, and although our flag did not tower over us as we would have hoped, it did not detract from our sense of accomplishment. Then we fed Mimi and Gray. We gave them a couple of apples. They were not very appreciative. There was a strong wind up on top of the hill. They were tired and cold, having stopped moving. They began to complain. Our victory was extremely short-lived. Anne and I looked out imperiously over the fields, savoring the moment. Then proudly, awed by the grandeur of the unmarred frontier that stretched out below us, we struck out on the downhill climb.

Mimi and Gray had already started to whine. They were tired and unhappy. The sun had come out, brightening the pristine face of the snow. They were now getting hot in their bundles of clothes. We didn't untie the ropes out of fear that they'd lag too far behind. We moved with them, laboriously, back across the broad, snow-blanketed fields. Once on the slick track of the ploughed road, we untied them and they trotted, weary and slow, heading for home on their own, like small sheep. But even before that, they had started to stink. We had smelled it faintly while crossing the flat white expanse of the fields, the sun burning above us. We sniffed, thinking at first that we must be passing a refuse ditch covered with snow, but the unpleasant smell accompanied us, and we realized that it was coming from the two little kids. They, too, had reached this conclusion. Feeling betryaed, they had both begun to cry. Their noses were running. They hobbled along, smelly, snotty, and near-blind from the tears that filled their eyes and glistened like the tiniest of diamonds on their chapped cheeks.

We walked on in front of them, horrified at what they'd become, while they ran behind us, trying to catch up. Anne and I reached the house first. We were hot and sweaty from our woolen clothes and our desperate flight from the two children who tagged behind us accusingly. We kicked off our boots, which were not without a smell of their own, and bounced into the kitchen, pretending a sudden interest in food. Ineko-san wasn't surprised. Our behavior was not out of the ordinary. She suspected nothing, although her nose wrinkled slightly when we entered the kitchen. But whatever the scent that had wafted in with us, it was faint enough to be only barely detectable. We were seated in the kitchen with huge bites out of our sandwiches, our woolen sweaters already drying near the furnace where Ineko-san had put them, when Mimi and Gray stumbled in.

The heavy front door rolled open to reveal the disheveled twosome, and at the same time, the most amazing stench filled the house. Ineko-san gasped and flew to the door, fanning the air before her.

"Ah, kusai. Mimi-chan, kusai, kusai. Mimi-chan, Gray-san, kusaku nai?"

She choked and grabbed the handkerchief that she kept in her apron pocket holding it over her nose. Anne and I fell back against the rear wall of the kitchen, horrified. Mimi and Gray, aware of the commotion and revulsion that they were causing, started to wail. Ineko-san ran to them and, holding them at arm's length, trying at the same time to keep her handkerchief over her nose, she began to strip off their clothes. Their boots, filled with a mixture of rank earth and melted slush, sucked at their feet and held them. It was all Ineko-san could do to keep from gagging as she freed their feet from those boots and peeled off the wet, smelly socks. Mimi and Gray were no help at all, whimpering plaintively. Anne and I were petrified, in total shock at the disgusting transformation that had come over Mimi and Gray.

They sniffed and sniveled, standing naked in the middle of the living room, such small children, looking smaller still with no clothes on, squirming like exposed worms while Ineko-san filled the bathtub with steaming hot water. Even their skin was malodorous, and they wriggled around in discomfort, waiting for the maid to come to their rescue, while Anne and I watched in guilty terror. Ineko-san grabbed them both, one under each arm, and dunked them together into the bath. They winced and whined at first under her vigorous scrubbing which seemed to pinch them to a clean, healthy, sweet-smelling pink. Silly things, soon they were laughing and splashing like a couple of hot, happy shrimp, blithely tattling, telling their miserable story, covering Anne and me with blame.

Anne and I hovered guiltily at the back of the house. Ineko-san, her nose pinched between her index finger and thumb, picked up the stinky clothes and dropped them in a big pile outside. Evidence. Anne and I exchanged ominous glances. Sara and Gene came home. They were not at all amused by what had transpired. The fact that Anne and I had not known that those mountains were composed of old sunflower stalks and horse manure fermenting into compost for spring did not excuse us. Mimi and Gray rattled on and on about what they had been made to suffer. The rope with which we had tied them was exhibited.

Anne got to take her skis and go home. Gene called her father, who came for her in his Land Rover. I, on the other hand, denounced by my two youngest siblings, remained to accept whatever punishment was deemed appropriate for the crime.

Sara and Gene decided to ground me. This meant that I couldn't see Anne for a week, that I couldn't even leave the house. It was not so bad when Samuel, Mimi, and Gray were out, but when they were at home it was horrible. They tugged at me to play cards and tell stories to entertain them.

Sara, Gene, and Ineko-san colluded with them, providing the games and the books, forcing me into a week of slavery. I couldn't even telephone Anne. By the end of the week I had cabin fever. I thought I'd go mad. Sara and Gene, on the other hand, seemed oddly refreshed.

One afternoon toward the end of my confinement, when Samuel, Mimi, and Gray were out, I was sitting in an armchair writing a story.

I could see Sara in the kitchen, over the counter, at the kitchen table, calendar, train schedules, and magazines in front of her. She was planning a trip to Akishima in March, at Grandmother's request. Grandmother's condition was worsening. She was very ill, but was still insisting on going to Akishima.

Standing at the counter with one of Ineko-san's blue aprons wrapped around him, Gene was making a big mess with a huge pile of shellfish, moving back and forth between counter and stove, cutting the heads off shrimp and slipping them out of their wafer-thin jackets of exoskeleton, pulling off runny blue veins, then rinsing them in a colander. They were shiny and gray, with big heads festooned with antennae and a pair of beady, accusing black eyes. It was actually the first time I realized that shrimp had heads.

For years, our dinners on Saturday nights were steak, salad, and shrimp cocktail, but the shrimp I knew were thumb-sized, pink commas, in no way related to living creatures anymore than a steak conjured up the vision of cattle. Heads, legs—these things were out of the question to me. Now, seeing Gene chop off those whiskery heads with a single whack of his knife shocked me. It also intrigued me. A strange tickle rose up in my stomach every time the knife fell. It was dizzying to think about it. Gene scooped up a handful of the shrimp heads and jackets and dumped them into the trash. Sara shuffled papers.

"Well, I think it's horrible," she said flatly. "It's like a witch hunt. It's so cruel. They're riding him out of town on a rail. The man is convicted and sentenced without even a trial."

"It does seem that way, Sara," I heard Gene reply. "But think about this: maybe he doesn't want the exposure. Think of all the old bones that digging of that kind tends to bring up. Maybe he doesn't want them to investigate further. Maybe there are other unpleasant things that might be exhumed."

Curled up in the armchair, I was only pretending to read my book. Sara and Gene's conversation was much more interesting.

"What do you think, Ellen?" Gene asked suddenly, as if he knew that I'd followed the entire conversation. "You know Mr. Graham pretty well, don't you?"

Gene, I thought, was starting to figure things out. He had a suspicious mind. I figured that this was because he was a sneak.

"Not that well," I mumbled. For children, recalcitrance usually works as the perfect diversion.

"Gene," Sara interrupted impatiently, "You know Ellen has always loved Mr. Graham's class. I'm sure she holds him in the highest regard, and I know she's going to miss him."

Sara's brow furrowed. She did not even look up when she said this. She had been reabsorbed by the schedules and calendars. Gene raised an eyebrow, whacked off one more shrimp head and looked over at me, the slightest of smiles on his lips. He couldn't hide it. Gene admired danger and narrow escapes.

I slipped out of the armchair and sauntered into my room, willing myself to show no reaction. Once in my room I threw myself down on the bed. I would really miss Mr. Graham. He was more than a teacher. He was a friend. I'd found some kind of balance with him. My perspective and his seemed to meet and connect in our peculiar fascination with things odd and troubled. Yes, Sara was right. I would really miss him. I wondered how he was feeling. I could see him sitting at his desk, head in his hands, Deshi no more than a shadow upon the wall behind him. I took out the curious Audubon prints, his gift, which I treasured. I settled upon the featherless, red-eyed face of a turkey vulture and studied it.

"Mr. Graham, Mr. Graham," I whispered sadly.

Later, when the house was quiet, Sara in Grandmother's room and Gene gone for a visit to Mr. Nielson's, I picked up the phone and dialed Mr. Graham's number.

"Yes," Mr. Graham's voice crackled into the phone.

I choked on my response. I had expected to hear Deshi's softly melodic Japanese greeting. The disorder was upsetting. Where was Deshi?

"Mr. Graham, it's me. Ellen," I managed to rasp out at him.

"Ah, Ellen," he said, his voice slow as the vapor of one of his cigarettes. "You've heard."

"Mr. Graham," I blurted out not knowing where the sentence was going to go, finding a block in my throat. "Mr. Graham, I'm so sorry."

"Oh, Ellen, don't be silly," he said softly. "It was my mistake. It was Miss Ibsen, the PE teacher, you see. What a fool I was. I asked her to dinner. Quite a mistake. A beautiful specimen, Ellen, just like your drawings. Absurd, however, to think that a dream and reality would have anything in common. I just didn't perform as she so dearly wished. Not a pass, you see. And so she blamed Deshi and my rather "perverse," as she called them, preferences. Oh, hell hath no fury like a woman scorned. Turned me in. Just like that. Blew the whistle. Made all sorts of accusations about my history. Implicated Deshi. It was all very ugly. Of course, I couldn't contest it. I'm guilty in so many other ways. It's justice."

"No, it's not," I said sharply, "I hate PE, and I hate stupid Miss Ibsen. Why did you even ask her over?" I whined. "I'm your friend. You have Deshi."

I heard the sigh on the other end of the line.

"A mistake," he whispered. "An error. You know, I thought for a moment, just one, that I could pretend to be normal. You know what I'm saying, don't you?"

Yes, I knew what he meant. I thought of the sea cucumber in its fragile glass prison. I thought of my own sense of hopelessness.

Then, quite a different question occurred to me.

"Are you in love with Deshi?" I asked.

There was a silence on the other end of the line.

"Don't be ridiculous, Ellen," Mr. Graham whispered huskily, "you know it's you that I love." He punctuated this with a self-conscious snicker that broadened the distance between us.

"What will you do?" I asked quietly.

"Oh, I will leave. Travel, I think. There is so much of Asia I haven't seen. So many places one can go, places where a man can disappear entirely. I've always been a ghost anyway, haven't I, Ellen? You sensed it. I could tell by the way you watched Deshi and me. Deshi knows it too. I am the one who didn't. Now I do. I finally know that I'm dead, the mere after-image of something that has already passed from existence."

Mr. Graham was drifting, even over the phone, becoming morbid. I was worried about him. "I'm coming over," I said. "I can't now, because I'm grounded. But I will as soon as I can."

"Don't bother, Ellen. You won't find me at home. Just the boxes. Deshi's packing everything. I will leave swiftly. No long sad departures."

"But, will I see you again?" I asked, the cloud of unhappiness blooming, pulling wet and thick at the front of my throat.

"I don't think so, no," came the dreamy voice on the other end of the phone. "No, that's very unlikely."

"I won't forget you," I swore, wanting to somehow fix him forever in a place where he could not be destroyed.

"As I am?" he laughed, "or as you have made me in your mind?"

"Both," I said hotly.

"Yes, of course, both. The artist. The strange, often imprudent artist. Good-bye, Ellen," he said.

"Oh, oh, good-bye Mr. Graham," I managed to choke out, long ribbons of misery delicately making their way down my face.

"Good-bye, good-bye, Mr. Graham," I sang sadly to myself as I hung up the phone, putting him away forever with the black receiver falling gently back into its cradle.

I heard soft footsteps on the tatami of the hall. "Ellen, daijobu desuka? Are you okay?" came Ineko-san's question, coupled with a look of concern.

"Yes, yes, Ineko-san daijobu, I'm okay," I sniffed, wiping my nose on the back of my hand.

"Yuki," Ineko-san said softly, pointing toward the thick mist of white that was swirling outside the window, surely mistaking my tears for tears of regret over taking Mimi and Gray out for their ascent of the mountain of compost and being grounded.

I saw the soft flurry of snow. It fell in feathers, laced itself over trees, bearding the pines—a fuzzy, swirling, soft cloud of white, covering everything, destroying it all as the white, like a great wall, climbed.

Bad things come in threes. That is what Sara always said, and that is exactly what happened. I was grounded, Mr. Graham was dismissed, but I didn't think about Sara's old saying. That's why I didn't even anticipate the third thing, didn't know it was forming while I brooded that day. I didn't suspect it when the small stones chipped at my bedroom window at night in the last hours of the last day of my punishment. It must have been close to midnight. Mimi was fast asleep in her bed, snoring fuzzily into her pillow.

The first little stone hit the window with a click. It could have been the wind. It could have been icicles breaking or snow melting and falling from the eaves. Then the next few little stones hit the window, one after the other—tic, tic, tic—a simple code methodically tapping out a message to come to the window. It continued until I couldn't ignore it. I tiptoed through the dark room and pulled back the curtain. What I saw made me catch my breath. The moonlight from the fingernail sliver of moon had cast all the snow in a pale blue moonscape against the black of the sky. It was so entrancing that I was completely taken off guard when David Vintner's face appeared at the window. I watched his mouth shape words theatrically on the other side of the glass.

"Open the window," he mimed.

I opened it quickly. The cold air rushed in. Our summer screens had been removed months ago.

David put his face close to mine and whispered into my ear. "Ellen, Ellen, get dressed and come out. I have something important to tell you."

"You're crazy," I said, thinking, *what a lunatic,* not trusting, fear catching in my voice. "I'm grounded. It's nearly midnight. It's freezing out there."

"No, it's not," he laughed, moving away from the window and spinning around, face turned toward the heavens. "It's wonderful. Come on, Ellen." He rushed back up to the window. "Please, I have something very important to tell you."

I think it was the tone of his voice, the brightness of his eyes, the way his narrow white face seemed to be blue, hard, and glittery like the moonlit snow. Maybe it was the week of being confined, or the cold pulling up around the sash and the clean smell of night stealing into the room.

"Okay, okay," I heard myself saying. "Just wait right there and I'll be out." I dressed carefully, not wanting the cold to lay an icy grip on me, finding ways to lock in the stored warmth of bed and blanket. I tiptoed through the house, while everyone slept, wrapped like dreamy chrysalises in their cocoons of warmth. But, as soon as I opened the front door the chill reached in and slapped me, a hand to each cheek where the blood rushed in with warmth, staining them, I imagined, very bright red. Then it entered my mouth, filling my lungs with icy splinters of cold, and the heat escaped in a fine steam from my nostrils and lips.

"David," I said as the steamy breath gushed out. "Are you nuts?"

David's eyes were bright. They caught the moonlight. He was very excited.

"Ellen," he whispered, grabbing my hands, "I came to say good-bye. I'm leaving."

The words sat outside my mind and waited patiently for me to give them the command to enter. But I couldn't let them. Something about them was too much. I chose to focus on something else to distract me.

"David, you have gloves?" I said noticing that my own gloved hands were surrounded by his leather-clad ones.

"Yeah," he said proudly. "Nice. From Tad. That's what I wanted to tell you about."

David was pulling on me. We waded through the snow-covered yard toward the back of the house through the rickety white picket gate propped open for the season by a drift of snow. The baseball field had become a winter amusement park where the trampled snow formed paths that circled and ended in snowmen. Melting stockpiles of snowballs that the boys had amassed had turned to ice. The ruined shell of Mimi's igloo hunched in the center of the field.

I was complaining bitterly. "Look, David, this is crazy. It's freezing out here." The hem of my nightgown, which stuck out from under my coat and below the line of my boots, was soaked through. I had on a hood, but the wind wormed its way through the outer layer of my clothing and now had its icy hands on my body.

"Yeah, but it'll be warm here," David said, pulling me down with him against the unbroken half-shell of the igloo. "See."

David put his arms around me. Then he said with a drunken grin on his face, "Isn't that better?"

I nodded, shocked out of my mind, surprised to be sitting there in the shell of an igloo with this dangerous, beautiful boy with his arms around me. *What if you were marooned on the moon at midnight in the arms of David Vintner,* I asked myself, supplying the opening line to that favorite game that had somehow wormed its way into the real world. I was brilliantly happy, but at the same time horrified, sensing that something was terribly wrong.

"Tad," David continued his story. "Tad, this guy. He's my friend. He's been helping me out, spending time with me. Ellen, he knows my dad, too. Says he knew him fifteen years ago, met him in school."

"David, do you mean he knows where your dad is?" I asked, suddenly thinking I'd made sense out of the bits of information David was sharing.

"Well, no, not exactly," David stammered. "But, I'll find that out later. What's important is this: Tad's in Tokyo now, and that's where I'm going. I'm leaving, Ellen. I'm going to find Tad. He'll let me stay with him. And then, who knows? Maybe we'll hang out together for a while. Maybe I'll find my dad."

What about your mother? What about Claire? I thought. I was glad those words did not come out of my mouth. There was no place for them in the igloo. They would have melted away the moonscape around us, destroying the thin bridge of ice that now, for the moment, joined David and me. Instead I said, "I'm going to miss you, David."

David's grip tightened around me. Bloated by our layers of clothing, we clung to one another like a couple of ticks.

"I'll miss you too, Ellen," he said gently, his eyes bright, exploring my face, resting on my mouth.

Then his mouth was on mine, and I felt his sorrow—the sobs that I wouldn't hear this time entering my mouth and falling into my throat. I closed my eyes, and we were spinning around and around, giddy music box dancers under the revolving constellations. I caught my breath. He took off his gloves, put his warm hands on my cheeks and squeezed my face. He squeezed so hard that tears came to my eyes. I felt a couple of errant drops start from the inner corners.

"All this shit about growing up," David said to those teardrops. "It's hard isn't it? No, it's worse. It's perpetually fucked. I hate being a kid. It's the worst part of life. You, you'll be fine, Ellen. You're pretty tough. You've got Sara, and you've got Gene. They're pretty good parents. Well, at least they care."

"But, what about you, David?" I asked, talking from the pinched shape of my mouth, not at all discomforted by it. Wondering when he'd let go of my face.

I must have looked funny talking out of a pinched mouth like that.

"Oh, sorry," he said, releasing his grip. "Me? I'll be fine, too. Better than here. They're killing me here, Ellen. I just have to go. My mom," he laughed, "she's used to guys running off on her. And Claire, well you know she's much better off without me around.

"I'll tell you who I'm going to really miss, though. I'm going to miss you and your family. I wish I were one of you. That would be nice."

Okay, so marry me, I wanted to say. *We'll grow up together and marry, and neither of us will ever be lonely again.*

But David, teeth chattering, was already struggling to his feet, replacing his gloves, brushing the snow from his jeans. He stretched out a hand and pulled me up next to him.

"I wish we were older," he said.

"Me, too," I replied.

Then David hauled back and with one banshee whoop kicked down the last side of the igloo.

"My next house will be bigger."

"Mine, too," I agreed, then we rampaged our way through the field, kicking down snowmen, everything, until we reduced all the structures to rubble.

"Hey, Ellen," David called as I slipped back inside my parents' house. "Thanks. Thanks for coming out."

"Oh, yeah, sure. Later."

"Later," he said.

Two days later—curfew lifted—we all heard the news that David Vintner had disappeared. They were looking for him, of course, looking for clues as to his whereabouts. Sara and Gene were very concerned. They liked David. They were worried about him.

"The Vintner boy has disappeared," they said.

They quizzed us about whether we knew where he might be. Samuel was questioned most closely. If he'd heard anything, he gave nothing away.

Sara's eyes were full of concern. She looked at me.

"Ellen, you don't know where he is, do you?"

I thought about David, heading south, toward Tokyo however he could get there, for a rendezvous with someone he hardly knew. "No," I answered squarely. "I don't know where he is." And it was a fact.

14

shinnen |
new year

It was New Year's Day. A lion had come to our door.

Click. Click. Click.

His fanged jaw snapped open and shut.

Click. Click. Click.

He was dancing to the music of four musicians. His large, red body undulated. His golden beard and whiskers wagged. His big eyes bulged under his bushy brows, and his head bobbed this way and that.

I saw Peganne, Ryan, Claire, and the twins gathered in the carport behind him. He'd already made an appearance at each of their homes, and they'd followed him here. Like cobra-charmed creatures or rats pursuing a piper, they were mesmerized by his dance.

Ineko-san filled Mimi's arms with oranges.

"Give them to the lion and the musicians," Sara said. "They'll bring you good luck."

"Wow, he really looks real, even though it's only two men in a costume," Samuel observed. Mimi cast a condemning look his way. Just last month Samuel had explained to Mimi that Santa was only a myth. Mimi still hadn't forgiven him for that. I couldn't fault Samuel, since I was the one who, years ago, had done the same thing to him.

"Why is the lion here, Sara?" Gray asked, ignoring Samuel's revelation that the lion wasn't real.

"He's here to drive out the evil spirits," Sara answered. "He'll go to every house. You don't want to miss him. The year will be bad."

I ran to the back of the house.

"Obaachan," I said breathlessly, entering Grandmother's room. As usual, I was shocked by the cold. It was like walking into a freezer.

"Grandmother, the lion, you must come and see."

Grandmother was lying in bed. She put one hand over her heart and held up the other, palm toward me, in a gesture of warning and closed her eyes.

"But Grandmother, if you don't come, the year won't be lucky."

She opened her lidless black eyes and stared at me, angrily pushing her open palm toward me. Her gesture was loaded with meaning, more eloquent than words could have been.

"Enough," she said simply. "Enough."

"I just wanted . . ." I started to say, but I saw the samurai-set in her mouth and jaw. It would be like arguing with a sword.

"I just wanted you to have a good year," I mumbled, backing my way out of the room.

She's going to die, I thought. Then with a rising fury, *She wants to die.*

I felt frustrated and angry. I was confused. I didn't know what to do. "I'll show her," I said aloud, going to the fruit bowl in the kitchen and grabbing the fattest orange I could.

When I got to the door, the drums were still pounding and the cymbals crashing. No evil spirit would hang around in that racket. Mimi, Samuel, and Gray were dancing around with the lion. Sara had tipped the musicians and the lion men well, so the beast was cavorting mightily. The other children were watching with hungry eyes, wishing their turns were not over. The lion, I'm sure, had not danced so well or so long for them.

I ran up to the lion and thrust my orange into its mouth.

"This is for my Obaachan," I said. "She can't be here. Make her lucky."

The dragon held the fat fruit in its mouth.

Its head cocked from one side to another. Its pop-eyes seemed full of surprise.

"Look," Samuel said. "He looks like he is going to choke."

The lion staggered backward. Its back rose and fell like a big wave. Then, the tempo of all the bells and cymbals and drums increased and the lion started moving faster and faster. It was twisting and jumping to the crash of the cymbals. It was writhing and leaping and shaking all over to the maddening beat of the drums.

It made two quick leaps in which both of the men inside were simultaneously in the air. Then, it fell to its knees and in a split second, the orange vanished into its maw.

We all stood there in silence, mouths open. Then we burst into ear-splitting applause.

"Hontoni sugoi!" Ineko-san said, sucking in air in a strange, hissing way when she said it.

"Yes," Sara agreed. "It's the best performance I've ever seen."

"And it was at our house," Samuel and Gray screamed gleefully. "Wasn't that lion fantastic?"

They were leaping around, not unlike the lion. Mimi was overwhelmed, but she too experimented with a few high kicks of her own. Everyone was satisfied. But I watched the departing back of the two men in costume with a sinking feeling, knowing one man was holding an orange, that the whole show was only a sham, sure that the luck wouldn't hold.

As soon as the lion was out of sight, Mimi grabbed Sara's hand.

"Sara, Sara," she begged, "can we have mochi nooooow?" She whined out the "now" in a long, nasal song.

Sara had promised Mimi that Ineko-san would toast the glutinous rice cakes, a traditional New Year's treat, on the family hibachi, a wood stove with the size and shape of an oil drum, that occupied a tiled space between the parlor and kitchen. It was also our only source of heat in the winter. Sara was always reminding us not to touch it when it got hot. She told us that blisters would rise and bubble if we touched it, and the skin would come off our hands.

Mimi wanted the mochi because Ineko-san told her that her rabbit had gone to the moon. The Japanese say there's a hare in the moon and that it has a mortar and pestle with which it makes mochi or "mooncakes." Ineko-san told Samuel, Mimi, and Gray that the rabbit had gone to the moon and was making mochi for Mimi. That's why Mimi wanted the mochi. She thought it was a gift from her rabbit. Every night, Mimi stood at the window and studied the moon, trying to see her rabbit. When the moon got full, she thought she could see it making the mochi for her. I didn't see any sign of a rabbit in the silvery orb overhead. It looked like a mirror to me, a round one with an old woman imprisoned inside it. I imagined my grandmother trapped in the moon.

The mochi looked like small blocks of white tallow. Ineko-san put the translucent rectangles on top of the stove. The white surface bubbled and popped on the glowing red metal. She turned each gummy block over. Molasses-brown blisters rose from the part that had been on the stove. Mimi, Samuel, and Gray exchanged cautious glances. It was just as Sara had described it. That was how they imagined their hands would look if they put them on top of the stove.

"Remember, children, this is a typical New Year's food," Sara was saying. "First we toast the mochi, then when it's finished, we dip it in soy sauce. Taste it. You can have more if you like it."

The mochi really did look like small pieces of the moon. It was faintly sweet, very subtle. It was just as we thought the moon should taste. Dipped in the soy sauce, the ghostly white cakes quickly soaked up the brown liquid. It absorbed the flavor like a sponge, the salty taste seeping into its rubbery center. With it, we also ate roasted chestnuts, golden ozoni broth, stars of lotus, and chrysanthemum blossoms. We each had to eat a bit of raw daikon radish, although none of us liked it. It was bitter. Sara said it made the mochi digestible. But, Mimi loved the mochi in its soyu bath. She ate it until Sara said she couldn't have any more, and even though her belly swelled and she was painfully full, she made sure that Ineko-san saved some for her for dinner.

Later that day, I was summoned to Grandmother's bedroom. I thought I was in trouble for trying to make her see the lion.

"Ellen," Sara said when I entered, "your grandmother has a gift for you, a very generous gift."

I could see in the dim light of Grandmother's room that one of her tea chests was open. The chair that I usually sat in was stacked with white, tissue-wrapped packages. Ineko-san opened one carefully, but not carefully enough. A long slip of white silk slid in a quick liquid motion onto the floor. "Aaah," Sara and Ineko-san sighed, as it puddled at their feet. The packages were full of Chinese silks and brocades, of alabaster satin and ivory charmeuse. They were full of slips, chemises, tap pants, and camisoles, of handmade nightgowns and embroidered shawls.

Ineko-san and Sara opened a few of the packages.

"Grandmother wants you to have this trousseau of beautiful things," Sara said. They were made for her, and they're heirlooms."

Sara looked sad. She was worried about her mother. I didn't want those old things. They seemed freighted with sorrow. They had strings attached. They were trouble. I wasn't the right person for Grandmother's stuff. But, I knew I shouldn't express this.

"Thank you, Grandmother," I said, feeling miserable.

"Here, Ellen," Sara said, handing me an armful of the tissue-wrapped parcels.

I sensed she was trying to brush them aside the way one tries to brush off a troublesome spirit.

"Take them to your room. Your grandmother and I want to talk."

They were lovely things, but I didn't want them; I didn't want what came with them. I didn't want the responsibility. I didn't want Grandmother's legacy. But I dutifully gathered up the packages and took them to my room.

Mimi, on the other hand, loved them.

"Put this on, Ellen," she said, holding up a pair of tap pants. "Put this on, too," she said, holding up a shawl. I could see that Mimi was terribly fond of the shawl. It must have reminded her of her blanket.

"That shawl is yours, Mimi," I said. "I can't just give it to you outright, because they'd probably get angry, but I'm letting you know it's unofficially yours. In fact, Mimi, all these things are. I'm giving them all to you. You just have to grow into them. Go ahead, Mimi, put on the shawl."

"Oh," Mimi said, standing on the bed with the shawl on. "Ellen, it's beautiful."

Then she looked at me hard. "No one's ever given me anything like this before."

"It's our secret," I said.

"I love you, Ellen," Mimi whispered hotly, pressing her simian-like body against mine. "I love you more than anyone else."

Mimi's love scared me. All her loneliness and neglect rushed toward me. It was so much. I couldn't explain to her that I felt the same way. That there was no one there for me, either, to be vulnerable with.

"I love you, Mimi," I said, feeling her hot, damp body and breathing in the sweaty smell of her hair. *She needs a bath,* I thought, seeing myself in the bathroom with her, telling her a story, the steam curling around us.

"Let's dress up and sneak mochi," Mimi suggested.

That's just what we did. We sat in the bedroom, eating mochi in Grandmother's underwear, and I spilled soy sauce on the spotless, embroidered white. I stood up quickly. Too quickly—my heel caught the hem of the garment and the tissue-thin silk of the slip I was wearing tore straight up the back.

"Oh, oh," Mimi said, her mouth full of mochi. "Whoops!"

"This, they won't like," I responded. "But they're not going to know. We'll just wrap this stuff up, and they'll never find out, and when we open it, I'll be old and you'll be old, and we'll just look at this silly old rip and laugh.

"Look, Mimi," I said, "it's just like a hospital gown. You can see my whole backside." I turned my rear end toward her and mooned her. Mimi laughed and I laughed. Then Mimi grabbed her shawl and started dancing around. I joined her. We finished the mochi, and Mimi fell into bed, exhausted. I tucked her in, then went to the bedroom window and stared at the moon.

The old woman trapped in the moon stared down at me coldly.

"I want Mimi to always be protected," I said to the moon, "to never know what it's like to be exposed and defenseless. I don't want her to be sad. I don't want her ever to suffer."

Of course, that was impossible, and I knew it.

jinja

spirit house

じんじゃ

15

amaterasu-ōmikami | the sun goddess

Amaterasu, Amaterasu-ōmikami, the Sun Goddess—her name sounds like a song. She and her brother, Susano-wo, who dominates the earth, and their sister, Tsuki-yome, the Moon Goddess, are the last three children of Izanagi, one of the two Creator gods.

Amaterasu and Susano-ō, the heaven and the earth, are the most significant of the Japanese kami—the Imperial line traces its origins to them—but it is Amaterasu to whom all hearts aspire. She is the most radiant, the most serene. She rises like the sun at the end of the long winter. She gladdens hearts. She makes the rice seedlings shoot heavenward.

According to the Kojiki, said Sara, Izanagi-no-mikoto, His Augustness the Male Who Invites, and Izanami-no-mikoto, Her Augustness the Female Who Invites, stood upon the Floating Bridge of Heaven and stirred the seas with a jeweled spear. The brine went koworo-koworo (curdle, curdle), and when they drew up the spear, the brine that dripped down from its tip made the islands of Japan. And they said, "Good, now there is a country." Then these two creator gods, brother and younger sister, descended from the sky and settled on earth, and began to create a host of kami. The first kami they made was set adrift in a reed boat. This kami's name was Hiru-ko—Sara said that Hiru-ko was the same as the god Ebisu, who was one of the eight scary statues at the Daimyô. The second kami they produced was the island of Ahaji.

Then Izanagi and Izanami made fourteen more islands. After that, they created a long list of kami including Ina-tsuchi-biko-no-kami (kami rock-earth prince) Ô-wada-tsu-mi-no-kami (kami great ocean-possessor) Haya-aki-tsu-hime-no-kami (kami princess swift autumn) and so on, until Izanami gave birth to the fire kami, Kayu-tsuchi. Kayu-tsuchi burned Izanami badly when she gave birth to him. Then Izanami, who was injured, adjourned to the underworld where, even with a decaying body, she gave birth to more kami. And Izanagi, who followed her, grieving, was horrified when he saw that she was no longer perfect and divorced her, creating more gods on his own, until he created three great kami—Tsuki-yome, Susano-wo and Amaterasu.

But from the beginning there was strife between Susano-wo, the kami of earthly tendencies, and Amaterasu, the kami of heavenly virtues. Susano-wo was disrespectful and destructive. He destroyed the neat boundaries of his sister's rice paddies and sent tortured animals to her serving maids to disturb them. In fact, Susano-wo so offended his older sister that she hid from him, locking herself up in the Heavenly Rock-dwelling. Then the whole Plain of High Heaven and the Central Land of Reed

Plains fell into darkness, and the result was so horrible that the eight myriads of heavenly Kami conspired to lure her out.

Ame-no Uzume performed a provocative dance. Birds were made to sing. Jewels and a mirror were tied to a sasaki tree, and Amaterasu heard all the song and laughter and gaiety and peeked out. She was most intrigued by the sight of her beautiful face in the mirror. Then the kami drew her out into the world, hurriedly barring her retreat back into the cave. Then the heavens and the earth rejoiced:

> *Ana omoshiro-shi* / *How good to see one another's faces!*
> *Ana tanoshi* / *What a joy to dance with outstretched hands!*
> *Ana subarashi* / *How revitalizing the music of nature!*

Sara told me the story, and looking around at the shiny green grass and deep brown earth pushing its way past the last thin retreating remnant of snow, I could see that Amaterasu-o-mi-kami, the Sun Goddess, was back. I turned my face up into the sun, enjoying its heat on my lips, cheeks, and on the thin skin of my eyelids.

"So that is the story of Amaterasu," I concluded, turning to Anne who walked next to me on the road to the bus stop.

Anne kicked at a rock with her boot, sending up a shower of slush.

"How can you remember all of those names?" she asked.

"I don't remember them all," I reported honestly. "I only remember those few. There are bunches more. There are hundreds of kami. Almost everything is a kami."

"Is that rock I just kicked a kami?" Anne asked.

"Yes, probably," I said.

"Is the slush a kami?"

"I don't know," I answered, considering the question carefully. "I'm not really sure."

"Well, if everything is a kami, how can you do anything without doing something wrong to a kami?"

"You can't. You have to be very careful," I said. "That's the point—do something wrong and some kami, somewhere, is bound to be upset."

"Well, I don't think I like that," Anne mumbled. "Are people kamis too?"

"Yes, kind of," I said. "I think so. At least they turn into kami when they die."

"Is a kami a ghost?"

"That's a good question, Anne. I asked Sara that."

"What did she say?"

"She said a kami was more like a soul."

"Nature has a soul?"

"Yes, according to Sara, it does."

"Hmmm . . ." Anne responded, sinking into silence.

We walked along without speaking for some time.

"It was a pretty weird winter," Anne said suddenly. "Mr. Graham being kicked out as a teacher; I missed seeing you; and what happened to David Vintner? He just disappeared."

"Yeah, pretty strange," I agreed, sidestepping the last question.

I hadn't seen Anne much at all. It was as if our enforced separation and the events that had taken place had created in me some barrier—like a river—and I was on one side, and Anne was on the other, and we watched one another from across the swift current. School wasn't the same with Mr. Graham gone. There were no more games about David Vintner. I was left with a collection of secrets—secrets I couldn't share with anyone, not even Anne.

"I think my grandmother's going to die soon," I announced, reaching out toward Anne from across the fast moving stream that divided us. "She wants to go back to Akishima. I think she wants to go there to die."

I didn't tell Anne about the lion and the oranges, about the old woman in the moon, about Deshi and the peaches, or about the notebook I'd lost and claimed was hers. I didn't tell her about my grandmother's trousseau, the half-shell of an igloo under the moonlight, or the feeling of David Vintner's mouth on mine. And Anne, without these pieces of information to help her understand, could only say, "WOW." And I watched the river between us widen as if swollen with melting snow, watched it become a tor-rent—wide, wild, and unbreachable—between my life and hers.

"I wish it were April," I said suddenly. "I wish all of this snow would go away."

Anne nodded, kicking up more chunks of gravel. Then her boot hit something matted and broad, sandwiched between the rocks and the mud.

"Hey, look at that," she said, digging it up with the toe of her boot. "It's a glove."

"Hey, that's Samuel's glove," I exclaimed, recognizing it from the double white stripe around the wrist. Samuel had lost the glove in November. It must have lain there under the snow all winter long.

"Not anymore," said Anne, sending it flying from the tip of her boot.

"No, not anymore," I thought, watching it turn from glove to projectile. Samuel had grown quite a bit that winter and the glove looked shrunken and pitifully small. "It's too small now, anyway," I agreed with Anne. "Samuel's grown up. It won't fit anymore."

"So much," Anne said carelessly, "for the glove kami. Au revoir, mon amour!"

"Yep," I agreed, admiring her soft, straight, brown hair and the way her thin chin pointed into the cold. Au revoir. Au revoir. Farewell winter. Farewell childhood. Farewell my dear, sweet friend.

16

jinja |
spirit house

"Ichinohe. Ichinohe Eki," the conductor announced sliding open the door to our compartment.

His face looked sharp, as though chiseled from glass. The dark light of the night coach collected on it and pooled beneath his cheekbones and eyes emphasizing their angularity. The shadows of the posts beside the railroad tracks bisected his face as we tore past them, turning it into an abstract mask.

Sara, Grandmother, and I sat quietly in the maroon velvet chairs of the train compartment en route to Akishima. Sara and I faced one another in the seats by the windows. Grandmother was seated closer to the door. Sara fussed uncharacteristically, arranging the woolen lap rug over Grandmother's knees. Grandmother's composure was absolute. She looked like a stone figure. Motionless on her lap, her pale hands were as limp as the waxy white heads of fallen camellias. She stared at me, but I don't think she saw anything. She seemed to look through me, to the wall beyond. It made me uncomfortable. I tucked my hair behind my ears and squinted through the ink-black sheen on the window, trying to read the shadows outside.

"Mama, daijobu desuka? Mama, are you all right?" Sara asked, alarm in her voice. Grandmother nodded slightly, gazing at Sara as blankly as she'd looked at me. The compartment fell into another silence, a silence that rested like a thick padded blanket on top of the clatter of the train's undercarriage as we flashed along over the track.

"We'll be at Sendai Station in less than two hours—tomorrow morning," Sara announced.

"How far are we from Akishima?" I asked. I had never been to Akishima, the family's ancestral home. I had no idea where it was.

"Not far."

Sara's usually creamy complexion looked sallow. It had the watery cast of weak green tea water. She seemed very tired. She and Ineko-san had worked hard planning this trip, acting on Grandmother's peculiar request, even though the old woman was not really strong enough to travel. It should not have been strange that Grandmother wanted to visit her family, but her illness suggested a darker reason for the urgency, and Akishima was so much a part of the past that any journey toward it, under the circumstances, could only provoke a shudder. Grandmother was not doing well. She had weakened visibly on the journey.

"Sendai Station on Sunday morning," Sara sighed as though promising us all a reprieve from the struggle. It was about as effective as lighting a match in a cave.

Grandmother seemed to surface then, as though from a trance. She seemed, at first, to be interested in the scenery outside. She turned to Sara and addressed her.

"Mado-o goranasai. Look at the window," she whispered huskily, nodding toward the window.

Sara and I turned to the window, startled by the sudden awareness of our own pale reflections bobbing back at us like a pair of eerie rice paper lanterns.

"Watashi ga mado-ni utsutte nai desho? You don't see me in the window, do you?" Grandmother asked.

It was true. Because of the play of light, Sara and I saw only the reflections of our own two faces pressing back through the window at us. The rest of the compartment was in darkness.

"To yu nowa kokoni inai kara. That is because I'm not really here," Grandmother said in the toneless chant of a somnambulist.

"Mama!" Sara objected.

"Hontowa watashi ga kokoni inai kara. Really, really, I am not really here," Grandmother repeated, ignoring Sara's protest. She settled back into the velour plush of the train seat, her bones arranging themselves one on top of the other and closed her eyes. Sara fidgeted nervously. She pulled a white cotton handkerchief from her purse. Only I was aware of her hands twisting and wringing the small square of cloth.

The train raced on. I tried to read one of Sara's books, but I kept losing track of the sequence. Sara sat the whole time contemplating the ebony void of the window. Grandmother slept.

"Sendai, Sendai Eki," the conductor yelled. Doors slammed all over the place. The train rattled and hissed to a stop. Grandmother awoke gradually. The clarity of only a few hours before had disintegrated. She was groggy and disoriented.

"Kuruma, kuruma. My coach, my coach," she mumbled.

Sara stood and leaned over her and removed the lap rug.

"Mama, mama," she whispered, "You must wake up."

"Akabo o yobinasai. Kuruma no ho ga yoppodo iinoni. Call the porters, it's better for me to drive in," Grandmother grumbled, still insisting haughtily upon a coach. I gathered our hand luggage and stood near the compartment door in my short blue coat, my hair tucked neatly behind my ears. Sara continued to fuss over Grandmother, who refused to get up.

"Ellen, please fetch a porter," Sara commanded. Tardy departures are not acceptable on Japanese trains.

The porter arrived, a fawning little man who gushed a greeting, and who when he heard Grandmother's grumpy demands for her coach, disappeared in a flurry. He reappeared shortly with another porter and with a quick bow and a show of great dignity and sobriety announced, "Kuruma ga mairimashita. Madame, your coach has arrived."

The "coach" was a stretcher. Since Grandmother couldn't be raised, a stretcher had been brought to her, and she was placed upon it. She was not offended. Rather, she seemed quite pleased by the porter's sensitivity and understanding. She must have been very light, because the porter was small and his partner thin and shaky, but they lifted her without effort.

Sara hovered over the stretcher, her face ashen. Grandmother's head had sunk into the pillow as though it were made of granite. It seemed that she couldn't raise it.

"Heya-o yoi shinasai. Have the station master prepare a room," she snapped.

The porters navigated the stretcher through the narrow train corridor. Sara and I followed along. Sara carried only a furoshiki, a silk scarf wrapped around gifts for the family.

On the station platform we stood for a while, disoriented, the porters aimless, not knowing where to go. Sendai Station, so early in the morning, seemed deserted. The sigh of trains pushing in and out of the yard was doleful. The station master came puffing up, and with great deference, escorted us through the station to his own rooms where a fresh bed had been made up on the futons for Grandmother. A doctor, he explained, had been sent for. I dropped our carry-on bags at the door. Grandmother asked for Sara's help to rise and go to the bathroom. She was taller than Sara, but as she leaned against her shoulder, it seemed that she was incredibly light and that Sara's struggle was not to support her, but to prevent her from floating away. They stopped at the bathroom entrance and Grandmother, leaning against the door frame, disentangled herself from Sara's grasp, entered the room, and closed herself in. She did not come out for a very long time. Sara waited. I watched how she waited as minutes ground themselves into dust. I caught myself holding my breath, inhaling now and again in gasps, like a person in danger of drowning. The platinum face of Sara's watch kept flashing at me. She smoked one cigarette, then another, and then she began to pace. Finally, frowning, she drew herself up and knocked softly on the door of the station master's bathroom.

"Mama, mama, daijobu desuka? Mama, mama are you all right?"

No response came from within. Then the click of a lock. We all heard it. The door opened slowly, and Grandmother stood in the doorway, her face gaunt, her thin arm raised, hand clutching the door frame to steady herself.

"Sekasanaide okure. Do not hurry me," she said deliberately, her eyes narrow with warning. "Saho o wakimaenasai. You must never forget your manners."

Then she folded herself onto Sara's shoulder, and Sara helped her to the bed, settling her onto the thick pad of the futons. I stood stiffly at the station master's door, the luggage piled up around me.

"Sara-chan, kochira e. Come closer," Grandmother whispered, addressing my mother but glancing over at me. She looked as if she could see right into my heart. I shifted positions, feeling very uncomfortable. "Sara," she said, switching to English, "from this point on, you are American."

"Mama, are you all right? Should we wait and go on tomorrow?" Sara asked pointlessly.

I was standing without movement, my lips and eyes repeating flat horizontals, intently watching Grandmother.

"I would like a glass of water now, yes, a drink of water, please," she calmly informed Sara.

Sara went to the drinking cooler and filled a small paper cup. I wondered if she had noticed how Grandmother's fingernails had turned a deep violet color or the dark thumbprint shadows under both of her eyes. Grandmother took the small cup and sipped daintily at the water.

"Anata niwa hontoni oyakoko o shite morattawa. You have been the most dutiful child a person could ever hope to have. Dômo arigato. Thank you," she whispered, her thin blue lips trying to form an expression.

"Sara-chan . . . " she said. She tried to lift her head as if she had something very important to say, but her head was too heavy, too heavy to raise, and instead it dropped helplessly back onto the thick wadding of the futons. She closed her eyes, as though she were merely resting, but she wasn't asleep. My grandmother, Hanabe Furikawa, had died. I felt myself poised on the brink of a precipice. What were her last words going to be? "Sara-chan . . ." Surely something intimate, endearing, consoling. But, Sara was never to hear them. She kneeled beside Grandmother's body, wearing the startled look of someone who's been slapped across the face. I saw a quick pain flash over her features. Then I saw her regain composure, harden, and close, again, the windows of her soul.

Because Sara said that she was American, because he thought she only partially understood, the Japanese station master handled everything. The doctor arrived. Gifts were arranged for all the porters. Grandmother could be taken no further by train. In Japan, no vehicle is permitted to transport a dead person on Sunday. This was a problem. The station master spoke a little English, and after much negotiation, a florist's wagon was commandeered for $3,000 in yen to carry Grandmother the rest of the way to Akishima. She traveled under a blanket of snow-white chrysanthemums, resplendent in flowers, back to the home where she had been born, where she was to be buried. My great uncle, her brother, a Japanese man in a dark kimono figured with mon tsuki, the sign of their house, and in hakama, black samurai pants, received her.

17

akishima |
autumn island

The florist's wagon bounced along in silence on the rough, gravel lane that approached Akishima. On either side of the roadway early plantings of cabbage, radish, turnips, and rice stretched across valley and hillside, in earthy brown squares neatly banded by watery ditches and dotted with green.

The byway became rocky, still more uneven. To the left, twenty feet from the road, an eight-foot stone wall rose and followed a course roughly parallel to the car path, dipping and climbing with the contours of the land. Above it, apple boughs poked out from the interior side. The dark branches were pricked with shiny green buds. A tangle of tall blackberry bramble, in some places as high as six feet, barbed the exterior surface. To the right, a knoll crowned with a big tree stump, backed by orchards and, past these, a thick forest of pine, dominated the landscape. Regarding it, Sara remarked wistfully that they had hacked down the three-hundred-year-old persimmon tree that she had fretted under as a small child.

"There was a kami in the tree," she said. "Who would do such a thing?"

"A kami?" I asked, hoping to elicit a response, to lead her into a conversation. Sara's silence and distance disturbed me.

"Yes," she said. "You know, a kami. A spirit. When I was a little girl I used to wait under that tree for the ripe persimmons to fall. I was alone so much. The kami of that tree was my first amma, my nanny."

"Where was Grandmother?" I asked.

"Oh," Sara said with a pensive smile. "She was away. She was always away. She was with my father in Shanghai. But look at that, they have cut the tree down and the kami will be so unhappy."

"Maybe the tree was already dead," I offered, trying to console her. "Maybe the kami had already left it."

Something about what I said got through to Sara. She looked at me sharply. Then her face became distant. I felt her drifting away again.

"Maybe," she answered laconically.

By this time we had skirted the entire eastern wall and the road took a sharp turn, driving into the enclave that the wall surrounded. Once inside, the route became straight and unbending, leading inward past lines of budding apple and plum trees. Gravel gave way to loose dirt on a narrowing causeway that gave the impression of not being much used. At the end of this track, which was really more like a drive, was a meadow-like expanse of low grass and in the center of that—boarded by outbuildings, forest and garden—stood the house.

The house itself was an old-style dwelling, not the lordly fortress of a daimyô, but a rustic samurai homestead, made of wood and roofed in thatch. Still, it was grand. The large exterior doors were of dark red mahogany and the enormous genkan was made entirely of stone. Sliding interior doors led up to the central hall, a large room carpeted in creamy tatami, in the center of which sat a huge table surrounded by zabuton cushions of pewter-colored silk. The table was situated over a pit. Over one-foot deep, the stony floor of this pit was covered with ash, as coals were placed there in the winter to provide warmth for the house. The columns that supported the house, great soot-covered beams in the central hall, had been polished to a mirror-like blackness by centuries of women. Those columns disappeared somewhere into the darkness above us.

"Your samurai ancestor had a fight with a demon," Sara explained. "He vanquished the demon, but the demon swore he'd take vengeance. 'You can't keep me out,' he had howled at his samurai conqueror. 'If you close all the windows, I will come in through the chimney.' So the samurai ancestor had built his home without a chimney, and the smoke collected for centuries up in rafters. In this century, tired of choking on smoke for some silly old story, they finally opened a chimney. And the war came, and Akishima was lost in the war. But mother bought it back for the family. Who knows? Maybe they lost it because the demon had finally found his way in, because they had opened a chimney."

I looked up into the rafters to where the chimney had been cut and tried to imagine a demon hurling himself down through the narrow opening. I tried to imagine the demon's appearance. He would be red and blue and golden, the color of flames, and he would leap and cavort the same way flames do. A chimney demon would certainly breathe fire.

But even with the chimney, the house was very dark, brightened only by the small windows and by the dingy pink and vermilions of the camellias and peonies that faded on the black lacquer screens in the corners. This house, like my grandmother's house in Tokyo, was muffled in silence. My great uncle, Shiro, the oldest of Grandmother's brothers and the only one who still lived on the land, was the man who had greeted us when we arrived. Grandmother had died unexpectedly. There hadn't been time yet for the family to gather. This man looked like Grandmother, tall and quite thin, but there was a depth and gentleness in his eyes that seemed to soften the severity of his manner. He was very formal with Sara—the two bowed when they met and exchanged no more than names. Every syllable of the names seemed to carry some meaning.

"Furigawa, Sakura," my great uncle said, using Sara's full name with a slow and precise articulation that gave it great significance.

"Honorable uncle," Sara responded, bowing in the way a flower bends when touched by a strong, late summer breeze.

Then, looking down at Sara, my great uncle had inexplicably smiled, and the smile seemed weighted with a profound sorrow and a profound understanding. I suddenly felt quite unlike myself. I felt as Gray might, like rushing up to this man to collapse against him in search of some solace— abject, overwhelmed, and unable to cope. But I am not Gray, so naturally I did not express myself in that manner. Instead, I bowed, and my uncle reached out and took my hands in his and held them, regarding them closely as if he were studying them. His hands were strong and warm.

"Kaze ga fuku," my great uncle said. Then he let go of my hands, told his servants to escort me into the house and turned, with Sara, to the florist's wagon.

What does "'Kaze ga fuku' mean?" I asked Sara later in the garden on the left hand side of the house where we stood, mesmerized by the fish that swam around and around in one of the fish ponds.

"Well, it means 'the wind blows,' in its simplest form," Sara answered. "But your uncle meant it a different way. He also meant we are carried away by the wind, that it is stronger than we are and that it presages change. In that way, he acknowledged a force that is greater than we are. That statement is the last line of an old expression. It is a form of resignation to the natural movement of all things."

"Oh," I said, pondering Sara's explanation. It seemed like a lot of meaning for three little words. I turned my attention back to the fish. There were three ponds in the garden in which large koi circled gracefully, silver and gold torpedoes moving under the green, algae-furred surface.

"They look like giant goldfish," I observed, still deliberating over all those multiple meanings.

"They are something like goldfish," Sara affirmed. "They are beautiful scavengers. They live for a very long time."

"How old are these?" I asked, trying to imagine what a long time was for a fish.

"Well, the large white one is probably twenty years old."

"Twenty years old," I repeated. I was only thirteen. That fish was older than me.

"Has it been in the pond all its life?" I asked.

"Yes, I imagine so," Sara said thoughtfully. "Just swimming around and around." Sara's eyes were far away, dreamy.

"How old was Grandmother?" I asked. "Wasn't she sixty-three?"

Suddenly it seemed very important. If a fish could be twenty, it didn't seem fair that Grandmother should live only until sixty-three.

"Yes, your grandmother lived to be sixty-three." Sara said this with finality. It sounded like a book being closed or a drawer being pushed shut. But I didn't want to shut the drawer yet.

"That seems young," I said irritably. "It doesn't seem fair." I paused as another question formed in my mind.

"Sara," I asked. "What do you think happens when a person dies?"

"I really don't know," Sara said honestly.

She was never one to feign knowledge.

"It's best to keep an open mind. Your grandmother, for example, hedged her bets. She practiced Buddhist, Christian, and Shinto rituals from time to time. I think if she'd known more about Hinduism or Judaism, she'd have practiced those too. I went to Catholic schools when I was a little girl, just like you. I suppose that makes me a Catholic."

She didn't sound very convincing.

"I don't know what to believe," I confessed. Sara laughed. It was good to hear her laugh.

"Well, Ellen," she said, "you are only thirteen. There is still plenty of time for your belief to find you."

Sara was holding something back, some deep truth. I could feel it. She wasn't really a Catholic. She believed in something else. I looked back into the pond and watched the big white fish swimming around in the shadows. I didn't know what I believed, but I knew it had something to do with that fish.

"You are a kami, aren't you?" I said to the fish. Then I cast a sneaky look over at Sara. Her faced was filled with a mysterious pleasure.

"Oh, I see," she said sagely. "Maybe you believe in the kami way. Maybe I am American, Ellen, and you are the one who is Japanese. How strange that would be. How thoroughly unexpected."

Grandmother's funeral was simple. She was cremated. Death is no good thing in the Shinto religion. That religion celebrates life. Death is a state that requires purification, so the ceremonies were Buddhist instead. Sacrifices were made to the spirits of the ancestors in the Shinto way. Family members arrived for the funeral. My uncles divided and redivided the land. Sara gave a big bronze bell in Grandmother's name to the village. She decided to stay at Akishima in respect and mourning until Grandmother's soul joined that of her ancestors. I tried to walk through it all untouched. The household seemed to be caught up in a quiet river of sorrow. When the somber undercurrents became too much, I escaped outdoors.

To the right, on the kitchen and bathroom side of the house, was a small well that the household used for its water. Beyond that a dirt path led back past the barn and stable, past chickens and ducks, to a small murky pond choked with blue stones, catkins, and tall purple iris. Skirting this, the path led directly into a large stand of bamboo, a fourteen-foot high wall of green that had been cut back to allow for ingress and exit on the opposite side. Upon leaving this bamboo forest, one arrived at the stone wall that surrounded the house, except that at this point, hidden by the rangy curtain of green, stones had been removed from the wall to create a gap that opened onto an almond orchard, two small stands of cherry trees, and field after carefully-cultivated field. The path skirted through the trees and continued weaving along on the margins of the fields.

The earth directly on the opposite side of the wall was wet, black, and pungent. It smelled of mushrooms and moss. A large number of the fields, dedicated to rice, had already been flooded to encourage the rice seedlings, and the shining surfaces of those paddies gave the landscape the appearance of an uneven green surface upon which a huge mirror had fallen and shattered. It was toward these fields that I headed, surveying the property and patrolling the boundaries as my Japanese forebears must have done for as long as the lands had been theirs. From a certain point on the far side of the paddies, I could see the village where the field workers lived and the backside of the wall that surrounded the dwelling as it rose and fell with the face of the land, for a mile or so, on its serpentine crawl back to the village. It was still too early for fruits and berries, and the rice was still young because, unlike the farms in the southern part of the country, Aki-shima would only have one rice crop each year. It was quiet out in the fields, so I roamed, unhindered, around the whole territory, exploring it bit by bit, charting its contours until I felt that, uncles or not, Akishima was mine. It was mine, not in the way that those yellowing old documents said, but in a deeper, more significant way. It was mine in the way the morning air rushed, sweet and apple-crisp, into my lungs; in the way new hay and manure filled my head with their sharp-scented aromas; in the way hyacinths opened like small stars in my heart and peeping quail filled me with curiosity and delight.

But there was one part of Akishima that I didn't explore, and that was the wooded shrine just inside the wall on the left-hand side of the property. From the garden and the fish ponds it was easy enough to follow the flagstone walk that meandered the quarter mile toward it, but this was a sanctuary to which my uncle would often retire, and I didn't want to disturb him. I wanted very much for him to like me. It was my guess that the best way to do this was to stay out of his way. However, snooping has always been one of my weaknesses. In the end, I simply could not overcome my old inclination to spy.

"Why does Uncle Shiro go to that shrine every day?" I asked Sara one evening. We'd been at Akishima for nearly two weeks. The place had cast some kind of spell over us. Sara still showed no signs of rousing herself from the trance-like world of her sorrow. She didn't even seem really to miss Gene, Samuel, Mimi, and Gray. I didn't either, but I knew they missed Sara, and I was beginning to believe that we would never go back.

"He goes there to pray, Ellen. You are very nosy," she added, regarding me with a stony glare.

It was true. I was very nosy, and that is why I followed my uncle and, crouching in a thicket of pines, watched him bow twice, very deeply, and raise his hands, palms level to his face, clap four times, and bow again after lowering his hands. That's also why, when he left, I entered the grove and did the same thing that he had in front of the shrine in which a kami surely resided. I waited, breath held. Nothing happened. I waited, hoping for contact with a kami, but the only feeling I experienced was a wave of certainty that I had actually done something terribly wrong. It grew—a tiny panic, ripening and swelling in my stomach.

It was a sour and sickening feeling. It bubbled into my throat and filled my mouth with a nauseating cottony taste. I felt like I was being watched by hundreds of eyes, hidden up in the pines, like the big eyes on the tail of a peacock. I closed my eyes and tried to inhale. The wind around me seemed to get stronger, seemed to move through the trees with a sound like a rattle, like a waterfall, like the dissonant clang of small bells. Then I heard a soft drumbeat, a gentle thumping that threaded its way through the sounds of the wind. I stood very still, listening intently. The noises wound around one another in a hypnotic way. They created a mystical music. I listened harder, bewitched by the sounds. It felt like the music was blowing right through me, as though I were riddled with holes. I realized then that the wind and my breath were one and the same and the timpani was my heartbeat.

I opened my eyes and looked up at the pines that towered above me. They seemed to look down on me in sadness. I felt like a prawn at the bottom of a very big bowl. The bowl opened up into the sky. The pine trees were nothing more than hand-painted images, climbing the gentle slope of its sides. Outside me, outside my body, the grove was so quiet I could feel the silence in a rhythm like the ripples that form when you drop a rock into the water. Silence has its movement. I lifted one of my hands and watched it float like a white cloud, past my face and out, settling downward at my side. My other hand repeated the pattern reaching out to the opposite side. Then I stepped and stopped with a little bend of my knee—in one direction first, then the other. The movement wormed into me, pulling like a string. I swayed this way and that, let my head go limp, a big flower lolling on its too-thin stem. It felt good to let myself drift back and forth like a petal tossed on a wind.

I had closed my eyes and behind my lids a dazzling white light was dancing like a silver koi. It twirled and swayed in the darkness. *The sun. The sun. It must be the sun,* I thought, opening my eyes.

Poised on the stone walkway that led into the copse, my great uncle stood, astonished, an expression of consternation occupying his narrow face. My eyes met his, and I felt my mouth open, but no sound came out of me. I looked at the great circle of sky above me, at the pines that surrounded the shrine. I looked at my uncle, at the thick carpet of grass under my feet. There were very few options for action. In fact, in my heart, I could see only one. My eyes found my uncle's and locking upon them held there, fiercely focused, like someone navigating by compass and star. Wary at first, then encouraged by the strong sense of clarity that seemed to be widening inside me, I continued my very strange dance. My uncle watched me in silence, then he, too, closed his eyes and turned, walking slowly back up the path toward the house.

A few days later Sara woke up from the lethargy that had possessed her. When Gene called and she heard the voices of Samuel, Mimi, and Gray, a look of alarm spread over her face.

"I miss my babies," she confessed, aghast, like a sleeper who has been roused from a coma and discovered that months have gone by.

In no time at all our bags were all packed. Sara communicated to my uncle her desire to go home.

"Stay, Sara," he implored. "You have not been here long enough."

"Uncle, I cannot, I miss my children," Sara said.

"Then I shall miss you," my uncle replied, acquiescing with a slight nod of his head. A sad smile tugged at the corners of his mouth, then resumed its position of waiting. "Please, then will you leave Ellen?" my uncle requested politely.

"Oh, uncle, I can't," Sara apologized. "Ellen has already missed far too much school. I'm afraid she has to go back with me."

"A pity," he replied, "but I think," he added, "she has also learned something here. So, Ellen?" he asked, addressing me directly.

"Yes, uncle," I responded, my eyes meeting his.

Sara stepped closer to me. I felt her hand on my elbow.

"Ellen has school," she repeated this time a little more firmly.

"Yes," my uncle said, closing his eyes and slightly inclining his head.

"Ellen, you will come back?" he asked kindly, moving closer to me, his melancholy smile forming for my ambush.

"Yes, uncle," I promised. "I will come back."

"We will be here," he said, and I knew he would, knew that Akishima would always be there, waiting for me to return. Sara finished her packing. My uncle showered us with gifts. I prepared for my final farewells.

I did not want to leave Akishima. Spring was stirring in the forests and fields teasing the land into bloom. Dazzling sunlight seemed to halo the farm lands, its brilliance mirrored on the shimmering surfaces of the flooded rice paddies. Following my favorite path, I crossed behind the well and cut past barnyards and stables, whispering good-byes to the chickens and ducks, to the black-maned horse, to the dragonflies and the water spiders squatting, pontoons afloat on the pond's brackish surface. Climbing out through the broken part of the wall, I threaded my way through the almond and cherry orchards, heading out toward the water-soaked paddies. It was quiet, the farm nearly unpeopled except for a handful of workers who waded through water-filled rice fields bending and standing, replanting the young rice shoots that were already thrusting their way up through the mud.

A woman with a child on her back and another at her side walked along the margin of the fields, headed home, probably to make lunch for her family. It was very warm out, and it felt more like summer than spring. "Time passes so swiftly," I thought.

I was picking my way along on the network of muddy paths that girded the fields, watching the sunlight ricochet off the water when I saw her. At first I thought she was just a mirage, a figure clad in diaphanous white flickering on the horizon. No one else seemed to see her. The workers continued their stoop-and-bend over the flooded earth, unaware of her presence. From where I stood, she seemed thin, but also quite tall even from that distance, and she appeared to watch me as thoughtfully as I was watched her. It was all very odd. I couldn't imagine why this woman in a flowing formal kimono would be standing in the middle of a rice paddy, but something about her struck me as very appropriate, the way a lotus looks floating on the face of a lake. She turned away from me as I watched her, and I noticed that her long black hair had been gathered, mid-back, in a ribbon. The ribbon seemed to be white as well, and her dark hair fanned down from the point at which it was gathered, falling far below her waist in a shining ebony column. She was actually moving away from me, seeming to glide over the watery surfaces of the paddies. She progressed for some yards then paused for a while, stopping to turn and look back at me.

She was very beautiful, shimmering there in the distance, like a lily rising from a swamp. I wanted to catch up with her and find out who she was. I started out after her, picking my way along the fields' muddy margins. The mud splashed up, covering my shoes in sediment, oozing into them and staining my socks. Meanwhile, the woman seemed to hang there on the water's surface, like a thing rooted, waiting for me. As I got closer, I could see framed in the jet-black wings of her long bangs, a kabuki-white visage. Her face was expressionless. Something about her reminded me of my grandmother, though she didn't look like her at all. Grandmother was sixty-three. This woman was young, twenty perhaps, the same age as the koi in the fish pond. She observed my awkward progress with the greatest of patience, as if she were used to counting time in centuries. Her lips were a very bright red. Pursed, they looked like a Chinese seal. Her eyes were like bits of dark glass. The sunlight poured over her in a halo of brilliance, but she seemed much brighter than the sun. She waited until I was only a few yards away, then turned and moved on, as if expecting me to follow. I did. We were far from the house. I wasn't sure where. The rice paddies seemed to stretch out in their endless watery jigsaw. The sun was directly above us. It was probably noon. There were no longer any workers about. The woman moved very quickly. I was getting tired of trying to keep up with her. And although she would wait, and although she was very compelling, I was ready to give up and stop following her. As if reading my mind, she stopped. She did not move until I was almost upon her. I got very excited as I drew nearer, stumbled on the muddy bank at the paddy's edge, slipped in the silt, and fell into the water, which came up past my knees.

Now that I was close, I saw that her feet did not seem to break the water's surface at all. Her kimono appeared to float over it. It was clear that she had no feet. I was shocked. I nearly fell one more time, my feet sliding again on the mud of the bank.

She was moving away from me again.

"Wait, Lady. Wait," I called out to her. "Are you a kami?"

She spun around quickly and faced me.

Her face was stern. Her hair glinted blue-black as a minah bird's wing in the sunlight. Again I was reminded strongly of my grandmother, although this young woman, with her starkly classical features, didn't really look anything like her.

She held up a hand as if warning me not to come closer. "Look," she said. "Namako. Look at you." She was speaking in Japanese, but I seemed to understand every word she said. In fact, it really wasn't like speaking at all. She didn't have to say anything. I seemed to read her mind.

I rushed forward, stumbling toward her, slipping again in the clay-colored mud. The woman moved back as if afraid to get near me. "Do not defile me," she warned.

"Wait, Lady," I pleaded. "Why are you here? Who are you?"

Shaking her head, she reached into the bodice of her kimono and pulled something out. It was a sea cucumber, and it was alive. She held it aloft like a talisman. It was wet. The wetness trickled down her arm and disappeared into the wing-like sleeve of her kimono. Then she spoke again. I was shocked by the intensity of her speech.

"Do you know what this is?" she asked, holding the sea cucumber high over her head.

I nodded my head 'yes.'

"Yes," she said tersely, without waiting for my verbal reply. "This is a sea cucumber. Namako. Na-ma-ko. Raw child," she added.

Her thin eyebrows, joined like caterpillars making an inverted "v" in the center of her forehead. "Namako, the world will devour you. Yes, the world will devour you, so you'd better be tasty."

The words burst from her with great passion. "You'd better be tasty. That way the gods will be pleased."

She closed her eyes and bowed her head slowly, as if waiting for some mysterious ax to fall. The sea cucumber wriggled about in her hand. Then she held it out to me, and I grabbed it. I could feel it struggling. It was slippery and powerful. It had a very strong smell. I gripped it tightly, amazed that it should feel so incredibly real when the lady herself was clearly a ghost.

"Lady," I asked breathlessly, "are you a kami?"

The lady regarded me narrowly. "Perhaps I am a kami," she offered reluctantly.

"Which kami are you?" I asked.

"Why?" she asked. "Why do you wish to know?"

"Because I want to ask you a favor."

"What might that be?"

"Have you seen my grandmother? She is new to the kami world. I'm wondering if she is there?"

"Your grandmother," the lady said, "is newly dead. She has not yet purified her soul in a way to join her ancestors."

"Can I speak to her?" I pleaded. "I have things that I want to ask her."

"Of course you cannot speak to her," the lady responded, apparently appalled by my audacity. "You are human, so dirty. Clearly, she cannot come near you. You hang on to that cucumber," she warned. "It's a gift, do not lose it."

I didn't really think it was such a great gift. It was one thing to study a sea cucumber, dead, in a jar, and quite another to hold one in my hand.

"It looks like it wants to bite me," I muttered.

"Don't be ridiculous," the woman said. "You are far more likely to bite it than it is to bite you."

"Listen," she said, "when the soul is pure, the water will always turn clear."

She said this quickly and with a great deal of feeling. Then she turned her back to me again and set forth once more over the paddies. Her retreating form quivered in the sunlight like a desert mirage. I didn't follow this time. I watched her disappear into the haze of the horizon.

When the soul is pure, the water will always turn clear, I repeated to myself, looking down at my mud-soaked shoes and socks, at the dirty wet hem of my skirt.

I was a mess, and Sara would not believe that I'd gotten this way in pursuit of a kami.

A kami. I had seen a kami, a beautiful kami, and she had spoken to me. Soon my grandmother would be with her, too, with the great rock-earth prince kami and the princess swift autumn kami. I would have to tell Sara that. Grandmother would be with the kami of the winds, the kami of the mountains, the kami of the rivers and ponds.

When the soul is pure, the water will always turn clear.

I chanted this to myself as I slogged back to the edge of the mire-filled paddy and clambered up onto the bank. Standing, rooted again on the slippery ribbon of land that bordered the fields, I suddenly felt as though I were racing along on my bicycle—going fast, very fast. I threw my head back to look up into the sky and then twirled around in a slow full circle scanning the landscape in every direction.

All about me spring was forcing its way into the world. Everywhere I looked, nature was exploding—robust and unforgiving. The tender grasses were already pushing their way up through the clay. Soon the fields would be green, and rice would cover the land. I could feel my own body stirring and changing. The pinch of the air, the stabs of bright green all around me were intoxicating. I drew several sharp breaths and realized, with a start, that the sea cucumber had, at some point, ceased struggling. I looked down at my hand in alarm, expecting to find a dead creature hanging there, throttled in my grasp. There was no sea cucumber in my hand at all. In its place I clutched a fistful of rice and mud. Rice and mud, what was that? It was Akishima. It was me. It was my grandmother's world.

I squinted back into the distance at the path that the kami had traveled. The shining jigsaw of water-soaked paddies swam together into a single bright lake that mirrored the sky. It was as if the pieces of a puzzle had finally fallen together. At that moment I wanted to laugh. I wanted to laugh and shout and run. I wanted to sing, and I wanted to dance. I wanted to celebrate wildly because out there in the fields, in the violence of spring, I had left the sadness and the severity of that ancient house and my mother's mourning far behind me. I had found a kami, a kami who filled me with hope for my grandmother, for myself, for every part of the world, one who promised that the water would always turn clear. It seemed I had finally found a trail through the lies and the secrets. I had found a place to come back to, and I knew, at last, the way that I must go to get there.